# Puppy Pals

Holly Webb

Illustrated by Sophy Williams

**LiTTLE TiGER**

LONDON

# Other titles by Holly Webb

# Contents

LITTLE TIGER
An imprint of Little Tiger Press Limited
1 Coda Studios, 189 Munster Road,
London SW6 6AW

A paperback original
First published in Great Britain in 2023

www.littletiger.co.uk

Imported into the EEA by Penguin Random House Ireland,
Morrison Chambers, 32 Nassau Street, Dublin D02 YH68

Text copyright © Holly Webb
*The Seaside Puppy* 2016
*Monty the Sad Puppy* 2017
*The Story Puppy* 2020

Illustrations copyright © Sophy Williams
*The Seaside Puppy* 2016
*Monty the Sad Puppy* 2017
*The Story Puppy* 2020
Author photograph copyright © Charlotte Knee Photography

ISBN: 978-1-78895-602-4

MIX
Paper | Supporting
responsible forestry
FSC® C171272

The Forest Stewardship Council® (FSC®) is a global, not-for-profit
organization dedicated to the promotion of responsible forest management
worldwide. FSC defines standards based on agreed principles for
responsible forest stewardship that are supported by environmental, social,
and economic stakeholders. To learn more, visit www.fsc.org

10 9 8 7 6 5 4 3 2 1

# The Seaside Puppy

For Eva

# Chapter One

"Are you going on holiday?" Max asked, whacking at a clump of nettles with a stick as they walked home from school along the lane. "We're going to Spain on Saturday."

"Yes, we are, but not until September, just before we go back to school," Jessie said. "We're going to Scotland for a week, to stay with my gran."

"We can't," Laura said, a little sadly. Almost everybody in her class seemed to be going somewhere amazing, but she was staying at home all summer. She gave a tiny sigh and peered over the bramble bushes to catch a glimpse of the sea. It was really blue, and the sun was making the ripples glitter. Laura knew they were lucky to live in such a beautiful place, but it would have been nice to go on holiday somewhere different!

"Mum's working," Laura went on. "It's the busiest time of year for her, the summer. All the cottages are booked up for the whole seven weeks. She says she's going to be run off her feet."

Jessie nodded. "Never mind. I'll be around until the end of August.

We can go to the beach. Mum's booked me some bodyboarding lessons for the first couple of weeks. I want to get lots of practice in."

Max snorted. "Yeah, you *need* the practice."

Jessie blew a cloud of dandelion seeds at him, so they caught in his blond hair, coating it in white fluff. It made him look about sixty years older all of a sudden.

"Oi, get them off me! Uurrgh." Max flailed at his hair crossly. "They're all itchy."

"Serves you right," Laura pointed out. "Just because you've been surfing since you could stand up, doesn't mean you have to be horrible to Jessie. She's only lived here a year!" She smiled gratefully at Jessie – she was really glad that someone was going to be around for most of the summer.

Lots of their friends lived quite a long way from Tremarren and travelled in by the school bus, so it wasn't that simple to meet up with them in the holidays. Mum had promised Laura that they'd try to fit in some fun treats and go to the beach together, but Laura knew how busy she would be. She didn't like seeing Mum so tired. Managing the cottages meant that Mum was on duty twenty-four hours a day, really, in case any of the guests had a problem.

Laura helped out as much as she could, although mostly she sat and did her homework while Mum was cleaning the cottages. But this holiday, now Laura was nearly ten, they'd agreed that she was old enough to stay at home while Mum was out. The holiday cottages and the little cottage where she and Mum lived had all been converted from the old farm buildings, so Mum would never be that far away. Since the beginning of term, she'd let Laura walk to and from school with Max and Jessie. Laura was even allowed to go to the beach for a little bit by herself or with friends. She wasn't allowed to swim on her own, though.

Mum had made her promise.

The best thing was that over the last few weeks, Mum had let her go to the village by herself to do some of the shopping. Laura had been begging for ages – after all, everyone in the shops knew her, she'd told Mum. It made a big difference, Mum not having to do all the shopping as well as everything else. Laura loved seeing her come home and look in the fridge, and say how nice it was to have everything done.

They were coming into the village now, and Jessie and Max waved goodbye as they headed down their road. Laura had to go on a little bit – Tremarren Farm, where she lived, was just on the other side of the village.

Laura sped up as she saw Mrs Eccles out for a walk with her Jack Russell, Toby. Mrs Eccles had been Laura's Reception teacher. She'd retired a couple of years ago and got Toby to keep her company.

"Hello, Laura! It's the last day of school, isn't it?" Mrs Eccles called. "Are you excited about the holidays?"

Laura crouched down to stroke Toby's ears. He was such a sweet dog, even though Mrs Eccles said he was really naughty and a terrible thief.

"Don't fuss over that little horror too much," she said to Laura. "He ate my breakfast this morning. A whole piece of toast! I don't think he even chewed it – it just went straight down his throat. Little monster, aren't you?"

13

she told Toby lovingly, and he sat
there beating his tail hard against the
pavement. He loved being petted, and
Laura was one of his favourite people.

"Oh, you bad dog," Laura
murmured, scratching under his chin.
"You'll get fat!"

"Luckily he goes three times as far as I do whenever we're out for a walk, what with all the dashing around, sniffing and chasing butterflies," Mrs Eccles said. "We're going all the way to the lighthouse this afternoon. He can work off that toast! See you soon, Laura. Have a brilliant first day of the holidays!"

Laura waved as Mrs Eccles and Toby turned down the side street that led to the cliff path. A lovely long walk all the way to the lighthouse with gorgeous Toby... She watched enviously as they disappeared round the corner. Walks were so much more fun with a dog. She'd seen Toby chasing sticks and Frisbees, jumping in and out of the sea and barking at the waves. Maybe Mrs Eccles would let her come along with them at some point over the holidays? Laura nodded to herself. She'd ask Mrs Eccles, the next time she saw them.

Henry padded uncertainly through the house, sniffing at the furniture. He didn't understand what was happening. He felt dizzy and a bit sick from being in the car for so long. And when they'd got out they weren't back home. They were somewhere else.

But at least Annie was here. She was rushing around with the others, up and down the stairs, throwing doors open. They kept shouting. One of the boys had tripped over Henry and then trodden on his tail – so now the puppy was keeping out of the way. Perhaps this was his new home, he thought worriedly, sitting down under the kitchen table in a forest of chair legs.

"Hey, Henry!" Annie crouched down to pat him. "Are you all right? Did you find your basket? Here, look."

Henry followed her over to the corner of the kitchen and sniffed obediently at his basket. Fortunately *that* was the same.

Annie put down a bowl of water, which he drank eagerly. But when he looked up she'd disappeared again, and his ears drooped. He climbed into the basket, slumped down with his muzzle sticking out over the dipped edge, and waited.

He wasn't really sure what he was waiting for. A walk? For Annie to come back and pick him up? He lay there, listening, his ears flicking. Every so often he thumped his tail on his cushioned basket when he heard someone come past. But no one stopped to fuss over him. Eventually, Henry drifted off to sleep.

# Chapter Two

"I'm a bit worried about that big group in the old farmhouse." Laura's mum sighed. "I've just been over to check how they're settling in. The whole house is in a mess already, and they've only just arrived. Bags and clothes all over the place! I don't think any of them are more than eighteen. They're having a holiday together because they've all just finished their exams, I imagine."

"Are they staying long?" Laura asked, pouring milk over her cereal. She was still in her pyjamas, looking forward to a lazy breakfast with no need to rush off to school.

"A whole fortnight!" Mum rolled her eyes. "I suppose it means less fuss changing over the farmhouse for another family after a week, but I do wish they were a bit more sensible." She sighed again, and then smiled at Laura. "They've brought a very cute little dog with them, though. He's a spaniel, I think. I'm sure you'd know, Laura."

Laura sat up straighter and peered out of the kitchen window, wondering if she might see the little dog.

The old farmhouse was the biggest
of the holiday homes, and it was just
across the pretty paved yard from
Laura and her mum's cottage. The
farmhouse was right next to the lane
that led down to the beach and it had
amazing views of the sea. It was always
booked solid in the holidays. But right
now the whole house looked quiet. All
the curtains were still drawn and there
was certainly no sign of a dog.

Mum laughed. "So you're going to spend the whole day staring out of the window to see if they go for a walk, are you?"

"No…" Laura said, going back to her cereal. But secretly she was thinking that it wouldn't be all that difficult to accidentally-on-purpose run into the dog and his owner.

Later that afternoon, Laura was shooting a ball at the basketball hoop in the courtyard when she heard a door closing behind her and a boy's loud voice.

"Come on, Henry! Get a move on!"

Laura looked round, wondering who Henry was and feeling a bit sorry for him. Then she gave a delighted gasp.

A beautiful King Charles spaniel was sniffing at the huge flowerpots on either side of the farmhouse door. He was only a puppy, Laura thought – he was really little. He bounced about on spindly short legs, yipping excitedly and whisking his fluffy ears. Mum had been right about his breed. Laura had seen King Charles spaniels before, but never a tiny puppy like this one. She giggled as she spotted his big ginger eyebrows. They gave his face such a sweet grumpy look.

"Oh, he's gorgeous. How old is he?" Laura asked, hurrying over to the teenage boy who was pulling at the puppy's lead. She was sure that someone who was walking such a lovely dog would be happy to talk about him. Who wouldn't want to show off a puppy like that?

"What?" the boy said, staring at her. His voice didn't sound very friendly, and Laura went pink.

"I-I just wondered how old he was?" she stuttered. "He looks very small."

"Haven't a clue. Come on, Henry, stop messing around." The boy tugged at the puppy's lead, and finally managed to drag him away from the flowerpots and out into the yard.

The puppy pulled back against his collar, whining a little, and Laura bit her lip. She wanted to tell the boy not to yank at his neck like that – that he was hurting him. But she wasn't quite brave enough. The puppy, Henry, belonged to this boy, or at least to one of his friends. She didn't have any right to tell him off.

Then the puppy seemed to catch the scent of the sea. He sniffed deeply and his ears twitched, and he followed the boy quite happily round the corner of the farmhouse, towards the path that led down to the beach. Laura watched them go, then slowly walked back over to her cottage.

Henry sat up and yawned, then peered over the edge of his basket. It was still much too large for him, but his toys helped to fill up the rest of the space.

He stared over at the kitchen door and heaved a great sigh. Then he nosed thoughtfully at his squashy ball, pushing it against the side of the basket. It let out a faint squeak and he patted at it with his paw – but it wasn't as much fun without someone to throw it for him.

Henry gazed over at the door again. Where were they? He'd been asleep for ages, he was sure. And he needed to go out… He'd had a short walk earlier on with one of the boys, just down the

lane a little way. There hadn't been
time for any proper exploring, but at
least he'd had the chance to do a wee.
Now he definitely needed to go again.
He knew he shouldn't wee in the house
– and there wasn't even any newspaper
down. But he just couldn't wait any
longer.

Henry climbed out of his basket,
looking around uncertainly. Then he
made a puddle and hurried away from
it guiltily.

He was starting to feel hungry, too.
It was such a long time since breakfast.
He was used to three meals a day, and
now that he thought about it, he felt
miserably empty. He went pattering
around the kitchen, sniffing for
something to eat. He scrabbled at the

door of the cupboard where he'd seen Annie put his bag of dog food, but it didn't open.

Slowly he wandered out of the kitchen and into the big living room. There were bags and clothes scattered around on the floor and over the sofas, and he wondered if some of them might have food in. One red handbag smelled delicious. A sweet, rich smell – much nicer than his dog food. The bag was zipped shut, though, and however hard he scrabbled at the fabric, he couldn't get in.

Henry sat back and looked at it. He was hungrier than ever now. He felt as though he could just eat the whole bag… He wagged his feathery tail briskly and crouched down by the side of the handbag, baring his sharp little teeth. It only took a few minutes to chew through the side and pull out a packet of biscuits. The plastic caught in his teeth as he tore the packet open, but Henry didn't mind too much.

He gobbled up the whole lot, then stretched happily and flopped down on top of the squashy red bag for a sleep. All that biting at the tough fabric had worn him out.

# Chapter Three

Henry's ears twitched a little as he heard voices and footsteps, and then the door banging.

"Look at my bag!"

Henry woke up properly with a start. Someone was shouting. He could almost feel the noise, as if the air was shaking. With a tiny whimper, he pressed himself down into the soft fabric of his basket. Were they shouting at him?

"That stupid dog! He's ruined it. Look, it's chewed to bits!"

"Oh, Molly. I'm really sorry. Henry, you bad dog! Bad dog!"

Annie had crouched down next to the basket, and she said the words in a loud, cross voice – not at all like the voice she normally used.

Henry whimpered again. It was definitely him they were cross with. But why? Annie never spoke to him like that. He quivered his tail, just a little, to show he was sorry, but she didn't seem to notice.

He watched miserably as Annie stood up and turned to the other girl, looking at the bag he'd eaten the biscuits from earlier on that day. She pulled out the chewed-up scraps of packet and sighed. "I guess it's my fault. He was hungry – I should have given him something before we went out. I'll get you a new bag, Molly!"

Annie put her arm round Molly's shoulders and led her out into the garden. Henry watched them go, his ears drooping. Those biscuits seemed a long time ago…

"I had a feeling that group of teenagers were going to be difficult," Laura's mum sighed as she put her phone away. "That was the lady who's staying in Rose Cottage. She said they were still out in the garden at midnight, shouting and playing music."

Laura looked at her in surprise. "I didn't hear anything."

Mum shook her head. "No, I didn't, either, but I suppose if we were already asleep, we might not have done. And the garden's behind the farmhouse, between it and Rose Cottage. So the noise probably travelled that way."

"I hope Henry wasn't scared by the noise," Laura murmured.

"Henry? Oh, the little dog. Is that what he's called?" Mum smiled. "I might have known you'd find that out."

"I saw one of the boys taking him for a walk," Laura explained. "He's so cute – he's really tiny. I don't think that boy liked him very much, though," she added, frowning as she remembered. "He just kept telling him to come on, and yanking at his lead."

"Oh dear… Perhaps it wasn't his dog." The phone suddenly shrilled

again and Mum pulled it out of
her pocket, looking at it anxiously.
"Hello? Oh, hello. I see. No, that's
not good. And you took him back?
Well, thank you. Yes, of course, I'll
have a word with them. Thanks
so much."

She ended the call and rolled her
eyes at Laura.
"*That* was the
family from
High Cliffs
Cottage.
They've
just found
a little dog in
their kitchen, eating
their lunch!"

"What?" Laura blinked at her.

35

"They'd left their back door open and he just walked in. They found him standing on the kitchen table, eating a plate of sandwiches."

Laura giggled. It *was* quite funny. But poor Henry! The man on the phone had sounded really annoyed. She'd heard him even from across the kitchen table and she was worried he would have yelled at the puppy. Henry had probably got a horrible shock.

"I think I'd better go over to High Cliffs and make sure everything else is all right," Mum said. "They were kind enough to take Henry back to the farmhouse, but they weren't pleased. And then I suppose I'd better go and talk to his owner." She sighed.

"You'll be all right here, won't you, Laura? Maybe when I get back we could go and have a game of table tennis." She gave Laura a hug. "I'm sorry, sweetheart. I was hoping we'd be able to spend some time together today, as we haven't really had a chance since school broke up."

"It's OK," Laura said. "I might go for a walk along the clifftop. Max said there was going to be a lifeboat display this afternoon, with a rescue helicopter. I can go and watch from the path. Though probably he got the day wrong, knowing Max!"

Mum laughed. "OK. I'll see you in a bit. Have fun!"

Laura grabbed her little rucksack and slipped in an apple for a snack, along with a water bottle – it felt even hotter this afternoon. Then she let herself out of the front door. Of course, taking the cliff path meant going straight past the farmhouse...

She was worried about Henry. That boy walking him yesterday had sounded really grumpy. And now the little puppy had been running loose! Surely his owners hadn't just let him out, had they? Laura chewed her lip anxiously. Either Henry had been let out on purpose, or he'd slipped away and they hadn't even noticed that he was gone. She wasn't sure which was worse.

As Laura walked across the yard,

one of the girls from the farmhouse came round the corner and smiled at her. She had very bright blue eyes and curly dark hair, and she looked really friendly. Laura smiled back.

"You live here, don't you?" the older girl asked her. "You're so lucky! I can't imagine living somewhere so beautiful all year round."

"It is nice," Laura agreed. "Pretty cold and windy in the winter, though. Are you here because it's the end of your exams?"

"Mm-hm. We're all friends from school. I'm Annie, by the way."

"I'm Laura," Laura told her, a little shyly. "I saw the dog who's staying with you at the farmhouse yesterday. He's so sweet."

Annie rolled her eyes. "He's mine. He is sweet, but he's been really naughty since we got here. I suppose it's just a bit strange for him, being in a new place. He chewed up my friend Molly's handbag – she was furious. And then this morning I didn't get round to taking him out before we went food shopping, and he went walkabout. Poor Henry. It's a bit of a pain that we can't bring him to the beach with us. Logan took him out for a walk yesterday, but he's been stuck here at the house since.

I think maybe he's bored."

"Oh but you can take dogs on most of the beach," Laura explained. "Just not Gull Cove – that's the part closest to the village."

"Oh, OK. That's the nice sandy bit, though, isn't it?"

"Well, if…" Laura gulped nervously, then decided that the worst thing Annie could say to her was no. "If you think Henry needs some exercise while you're out, maybe I could take him for a walk along the beach here."

Annie stared at her. "Really?"

"Yeah. I love dogs and I don't have one. I'd like to. Um, if you think that would be OK."

"Sure." Annie beamed at her. "That would be great. You can take him now, if you like? I'll go and get him."

"Oh!" Laura nodded eagerly. "Right now? Yes, please!"

Annie grinned at her and headed into the farmhouse, while Laura waited in the yard. She was so excited she was actually hopping from foot to foot, she realized. She went pink and put both feet very firmly on the ground. Annie wouldn't want her to take Henry out if she thought Laura was being silly.

Laura knew she ought to go and tell her mum, but she squashed down the thought at the back of her mind. Mum had gone off to talk to the people at High Cliffs Cottage, so she couldn't ask right now. And Laura was pretty sure Mum wouldn't mind. After all, she'd said that Henry was really cute, hadn't she?

Then Annie came out with Henry, and all thoughts about asking Mum went out of Laura's head entirely. He was just so lovely. He was peeping shyly round Annie's legs, looking up at Laura with his head on one side. A smart red collar and lead stood out against the black fur of his neck, and his white paws were spotlessly clean.

Laura crouched down and slowly put out one hand for Henry to sniff.

"You're sure it's all right for me to take him?" Laura said, as the puppy eyed her cautiously.

"Of course." Annie put the lead into Laura's hand and patted Henry. "Be good, Henry-dog! Oh! Nearly forgot." She darted back into the house. "You might need these. Poo bags." She made a face. "I know it's a bit disgusting…"

Laura shook her head. "No. I mean, it is, but it would be worse just leaving it for someone to tread in. Thanks." She tucked the bags in her pocket and looked down at the puppy. "Going to come for a walk, Henry?" Then she giggled as Henry's tail began to sweep from side to side, faster and faster.

He obviously knew what that word meant. She tugged gently on his lead and set off around the side of the farmhouse, down the path to the clifftop and the beach.

Henry followed, a little confused by this new person. But then he'd seen a lot of new people over the last few days. The house was full of strange, big, noisy people. Whenever he was settling down to sleep, or trying to climb on Annie's lap for a cuddle, someone would clomp by loudly, or fling themselves down on to the sofa.

He trotted after the girl, liking the low voice she was using to coax him along and the way she didn't pull at his lead.

The narrow path that led to the cliffs was a bit overgrown, but it smelled amazing to a small dog. Henry stopped to plunge his nose among the clumps of grass, shaking his feathery ears in excitement. He snorted delightedly, snuffling in among the weeds, and the girl laughed.

"Is that nice?" she murmured. "What can you smell? Is it rabbits?"

Henry looked up at her, wagging his tail, and then licked her hand. The sun was warm on his fur and the air was full of good smells. This girl wasn't hurrying him along like that boy, Logan, had the day before. She didn't seem to mind how long he spent investigating everything. He panted happily and headed on down the path.

# Chapter Four

Laura looked down at Henry thoughtfully. He was prancing along, although he did keep stopping to sniff at something every couple of metres, which slowed them down a bit. Even though he was so bouncy, she wasn't sure how far he'd be able to walk. She knew King Charles spaniels could be energetic, but he was only little – and she didn't think that Annie had been taking him on long walks, either.

"We'd better not go too far," she said. "Let's walk down the path to the beach. This is Warren Cove. I bet you smelled all the rabbits up on the cliff, didn't you?"

Henry scurried down the path ahead of her, ears flapping in the breeze. As the scrubby grass turned to sand and pebbles he stopped, lifting up each front paw, and then putting them down again, looking confused. This gritty stuff between his paws was new, his expression said quite clearly.

"Haven't you been on the beach at all?" Laura said, surprised. "Oh, of course – they thought you weren't allowed.

It's sand. Don't you like it? You can dig, look." She crouched down and scuffled a hole in the sand, just in front of Henry's nose. He gave a squeaky little yelp and plunged both forepaws in straight away, scratching madly and sending sand flying all over the place.

Laura sat back, laughing and holding up her hand to shield her face. "I'm going to have to brush you before I give you back – you're covered!"

The puppy's long fur was clotted with golden biscuity sand, especially in the pretty feathery bits around his paws and chest.

"Unless you wanted to go for a paddle, of course," Laura said, looking thoughtfully at the sea. It was beautifully calm today – a still, glassy greenish-blue, with little creamy waves breaking on to the pebbles. "Come on, Henry. Let's go and have a look at the sea." She jumped up, patting at her leg, and Henry trotted after her.

Henry slowed down as they got closer to the water and stared at it suspiciously.

"It's OK," Laura whispered, kicking off her flip-flops and

crouching down next to him. "I know, it's funny, isn't it? It keeps going in and out."

Henry looked up at her and wagged his tail uncertainly. He didn't understand what the sea was at all. But the girl didn't sound very worried by it. She didn't step back when it came hissing and foaming towards them.

Laura stayed crouching next to Henry. She hoped he would go into the water – she knew lots of dogs loved swimming. It would wash some of the sand off, too. And she couldn't help imagining how gorgeous he'd look, paddling about in the sea... She didn't want to make him, though.

Henry took a step forward, and then barked in surprise as the water made a rush at him, sucking the sand out from beneath his paws. It was cold! He shook his paws, then barked again as the drops splashed and sparkled around him.

Laura giggled, and he looked up at her. "Do you like it?" she asked. She couldn't quite tell.

Henry stayed put, even though the next wave came right up to his tummy. He jumped and barked at the ripples and the yellowish foam.

Laura was just thinking how much fun it would be to come down with her swimming costume on one day, so she and Henry could have a proper splash about, when a sudden loud roaring made her jump. She nearly slipped over, but then she clapped a hand over her mouth and laughed. "Oh! Oh, wow, a helicopter!"

It was flying round the curve of the cliffs that shaped the little bay and divided the two beaches. The tall cliffs had shielded Laura and Henry from the sound of the rotors until it came right into the bay.

"I guess it's on the way to that lifeboat display Max was talking about," Laura said.

The lead suddenly jerked in her hands

and Laura looked down in surprise. "Oh, Henry!"

The puppy was whining in fright, tugging frantically at the lead and backing away across the sand.

He hated the noise. He'd never heard anything so loud and he could feel the ground shaking.

"Don't worry." Laura picked him up, hugging the tiny dog tight. He was really scared, she could tell – he was shivering in her arms. "Honestly, it's just a helicopter. It was noisy, though wasn't it?" She went on talking soothing nonsense to calm him down as the helicopter flew across the bay.

At last it disappeared round the other side of the cliffs. "It's gone now," she said gently. "Come on, sweetie. Do you want to paddle a bit more?" She rubbed her hand over his silky ears and he snuggled against her, burying his head in her T-shirt.

"Maybe we'd better just head home," Laura muttered, grabbing her flip-flops and wobbling as she tried to put them back on without letting go of Henry. "I don't know if that helicopter's going to come past again." She picked her way slowly across the stones towards the steps that led up from the other end of the beach.

Henry wriggled in her arms as he picked up the scent of a patch of half-dried seaweed. Laura thought it smelled disgusting, but she supposed it might be nice if you were a dog. She put him down so he could rootle through it. At least it was distracting him from the scary helicopter.

Finally Henry lost interest in the seaweed and went sniffing his way across the beach towards the path. He was still a bit twitchy, Laura noticed. When he heard another dog barking from up on the cliffs, he jumped and pressed himself against her legs.

Laura went on murmuring to him as they walked up the cliff path – saying comforting things about how nice the hot sun was, and how she loved the sharp smell of the wild fennel growing along the path. She could see he was listening to her. Of course he didn't understand what she was saying, but Laura was sure that didn't matter.

They stopped at the top and Laura let out a great sigh. "That path is so steep!" She glanced down at Henry, who was panting, too. He flopped on to the short turf, looking tired and hot.

"You need a drink," Laura said, sitting down beside him and opening up her rucksack. She looked at her water bottle, wondering if Henry would let her dribble some water in his mouth. She wished she'd thought of bringing him a bowl. Henry was still panting, with fast, short little breaths. He sounded miserable.

"This will have to do," Laura told him, cupping one hand and pouring some water into it. She saw Henry's ears flickering as he heard the splashing sound, and he sat up eagerly. She held her hand under his nose, and at first he just looked at it, confused. Then he realized what she was doing and lapped eagerly at the water. It was gone in seconds.

"More?" Laura refilled her hand, giggling as Henry's soft pink tongue swept over her palm. "You really are thirsty."

Henry drank five handfuls of water, and then flopped down again. But this time he looked much happier. He was resting his chin on his paws as he watched the bees buzzing through the wild flowers by the path.

Laura sat stroking his back, feeling the sun on her hair and pretending, just for a moment, that Henry was hers.

"I'd take you on lots of walks," she whispered. "Of course I'd always bring your water bowl. And I'd never let a helicopter come anywhere near." She smiled to herself. As if she could stop a helicopter! But it was all just imagining, anyway. Henry was someone else's puppy.

"I suppose we ought to get going," Laura sighed at last. "Come on, Henry. It isn't too far, I promise."

Henry heaved himself up and padded along the grassy path after Laura. He wasn't as bouncy as he had been when they'd set off, but he still looked like he was enjoying himself. When a butterfly fluttered over his nose he yapped excitedly and tried to jump up at it. He didn't get anywhere near, of course, and he watched rather grumpily as the butterfly whirled away.

Laura laughed. "You are a funny thing," she told him. "What would you do with a butterfly if you caught it, anyway?"

They were almost home when a couple of seagulls came diving by. Huge white herring gulls with wide grey wings. They swooped over Laura and Henry, shrieking, and Henry squealed in fright. He was still a bit nervous from before, and the gulls had darted straight past his nose!

"Henry!" Laura yelled in panic as the puppy tugged hard at his lead and it slipped out of her hand.

She dashed after him as he turned tail and raced back along the path the way they'd come. He didn't stop until he came to a tangle of brambles, just at the edge of the cliff. The stems were thick and dark with thorns, but he wriggled underneath.

Laura kneeled down to look at him,

crouching under the brambles. "Oh, Henry," she whispered.

The puppy peered out at her and whimpered a little. Everything was different and scary, and he didn't understand. First the new house and all those people who kept shouting at him. Then that roaring thing had swooped over his head, so loud it had made his ears hurt. And now the shrieking birds. Everything felt wrong.

"It's all right…" The girl was talking again, so quietly. Her whispers were soothing and he crept out of the brambles a little, just close enough for her to rub her hand over his head and stroke his ears.

He crawled a bit further, plunging his head into her knees and letting her wrap her arms around him. She smelled good, Henry thought. His racing heart slowed slightly and he relaxed against her with a shiver.

"Poor Henry," she muttered. "Poor sweetheart. You're safe now."

# Chapter Five

"She really lets you take him for a walk every day?" Jessie asked, wonderingly.

"Every day for the last five days now. I'm so lucky. We went as far as the lighthouse this morning. That's a long walk for him, but he was brilliant." Laura smiled down proudly at Henry as he pranced over the sand in front of them. "I didn't think Annie would ever let me take him out again after the first time. He was all sandy and he had bits of bramble in his fur when we got back. But she went and got his brush, and we groomed him together. Annie said he seemed to really like me."

"Yes, but why doesn't she want to take him herself?" Jessie asked. "If I had a gorgeous dog like that, I wouldn't let other people walk him!"

"I suppose she doesn't have time because she's on holiday with her friends. I don't know – I'm just grateful." Laura sighed. "But I'm going to miss him so much when they go. They're only here for one more week. Of course, Mum can't wait for them to leave. Two of the other families have complained that they're too noisy, and she keeps worrying about what's going to go wrong next!"

"Oh yes, she was telling my mum about them when they ran into each other in the baker's. Is your mum OK with you going off walking him all the time?"

"She said it was fine as long as I tell her where we're going. But she was a bit worried when I told her about those seagulls."

Jessie shuddered. "One of them snatched my sandwich last summer when we were having a picnic on the beach. They're huge!"

"Especially when you're only the size of Henry," Laura agreed.

They both laughed as Henry stopped and turned round. It was like he understood that they were talking about him.

"Did you tell Annie about the seagulls, too?" Jessie said.

Laura nodded. "I didn't really want to, in case she thought I wasn't looking after him properly, but I had to explain all those bits of bramble in his fur."

"So what did she say?" Jessie asked.

Laura ruffled Henry's ears. "She said she wasn't very surprised. She should have warned me he hated loud noises, and it definitely wasn't my fault he slipped the lead. Oh, look, that's her," Laura said, nudging Jessie. "With the curly hair. I thought they always went to Gull Cove."

"If they were coming here, she could have taken Henry with her. After all, dogs are allowed on this beach," Jessie pointed out.

Laura shrugged – she wasn't sure

why Annie hadn't brought him, either. "I suppose he wouldn't want to sit still while they all sunbathed..."

Annie was lying on the sand and chatting with one of the other girls from the farmhouse, the one Laura thought was called Molly. Laura had met her when she took Henry back the day before.

Annie sat up as she saw them coming over and shielded her eyes from the sun. "Hi there, Laura! Hi, Henry!"

Henry scampered over to her excitedly, pulling Laura along behind him. He ran across Annie's towel and scrabbled at her, hoping she'd fuss over him.

"Ow, ow, claws!" Annie pushed him away gently. She was only wearing a swimming costume and he was scratching her legs.

Henry sat back, his ears drooping a little, and Laura crouched down to stroke him. "It's OK – you can't jump up on people, that's all," she said. But she felt bad for the puppy. He'd just wanted his owner to give him a cuddle.

Henry wagged his tail slowly as she stroked him, and Annie kneeled up and joined in.

"You're so good with him," Annie told Laura, ruffling Henry's ears.

"Thanks!" Laura smiled at her. "I think he's the nicest dog I've ever met. Jessie thinks he's beautiful, too."

"And really friendly," Jessie added.

Annie smiled. "I know – he's perfect."

"You have to be quiet," Laura whispered. "Mum's out, and I don't think she'll be back for a while, but just in case." She watched happily as Henry sniffed his way around her bedroom. He spent ages nosing at her trainers, and Laura made faces at him. "That's disgusting! Yuck!"

Henry sat back and sneezed, looking very surprised at himself. Laura laughed so much she had to hug her arms tight around her ribs to stop them hurting. His ginger eyebrows

looked as if they might lift off! But
after one last quick sniff at the trainers,
he went on exploring, scrabbling at
Laura's bin to see what was inside.
He had his front paws balanced on the
edge as he kicked and scrambled his
back paws up the side.

"Hey, Henry,
that's going to
tip over," Laura
started to say,
hopping up
from her bed,
but the bin had
already started
falling. Henry
collapsed on
the floor in a pile of
screwed up homework sheets.

"You do look funny, silly dog," Laura told him, stuffing all the paper back into the bin and scooping him up for a cuddle. "Come on, come and sit with me on the bed."

It was so hot today, too hot and sticky to be outside in the sun, Laura thought. Especially for a little puppy. So she'd retreated to her room instead. She was sure Annie wouldn't mind her taking Henry up there.

Henry snuggled happily in Laura's lap and she leaned back against the pile of cushions and soft toys. It was so warm, even with the skylight and windows open. Henry turned himself around a couple of times, yawned hugely and slumped down again. He still had that puppy knack of falling asleep in seconds, whatever he was doing.

Laura looked down at Henry lovingly and stretched out one arm to grab the book from her bedside table. She didn't want to disturb him, he looked so comfy. She'd just read for a bit...

"Laura!"

Laura sat up with a jerk, and Henry started to slide off her lap. As she grabbed at him, he snuffled and snorted and woke up, looking surprised.

Laura gaped up at her mum. She'd fallen asleep! They both had! She'd meant to take Henry home long before

Mum was due back. She hoped Annie wasn't too worried.

"Sorry," she said. "I should have asked…"

Her mum sat down beside her on the bed and tickled Henry under the chin. He wagged his tail happily and stomped across the bed to give Mum a proper sniff. Then he slumped down again, still weary, with his chin on her leg.

"Aww," Laura's mum sighed, stroking his ears. "But I'm still cross with you, Laura," she added quickly. "Yes, you *definitely* should have asked. And I'd probably have said no."

"Don't you like him?" Laura said, rather sadly.

"Of course I like him – he's adorable. But he's not yours. That's what worries me.

You've been spending so much time with him, and now he's in your bedroom – just like he's your own puppy! He'll be going home soon, and I don't want you to be upset."

Laura's shoulders slumped. "I know he'll go home with Annie. And I already know how much I'll miss him," she admitted in a whisper. "But at least he's happy here with me. I'm not sure Annie's looking after him very well," she added. "If I didn't walk him, Mum, I don't know if anybody would. They always leave him in the house on his own when they go to the beach. They could easily take him with them."

Mum leaned back against the cushions and looked at Henry. "It's really good that you care about him so much," she said slowly, "but there's not a lot we can do. He belongs to someone else. He's Annie's dog, Laura."

"People who are lucky enough to have dogs ought to take better care of them!" Laura burst out. Her eyes were shining with tears, but her fists were clenched and she looked more angry than upset.

Henry gazed up at her and hunched his shoulders anxiously. He could hear the unhappiness in her voice and he let out a tiny whimper.

"I'm sorry, Henry. I didn't mean to scare you." Laura ran her hand gently over his head, murmuring to him soothingly.

Henry padded round in a circle on the bed, and then scrambled back into her lap and settled down. He was still eyeing Laura cautiously, though. He loved her partly for her quiet, gentle voice. That high, angry tone was all wrong – he'd never heard her sound like that before.

Henry wasn't sure what had happened. He liked the lady sitting next to them, too – she'd stroked him and made a fuss of him. But then something she'd said had made Laura's voice go sharp. Now he looked between Laura and her mum uncertainly.

"He's very quick at picking up how people feel, isn't he?" Mum murmured. "He knew straight away that you were upset and he didn't like it."

"I know… I think he doesn't like how busy and loud the farmhouse is, either," Laura said, glancing up at her worriedly. "When I took him back there yesterday, after our walk with Jessie, a couple of the boys were shouting. They weren't fighting or anything, just yelling because one was upstairs and one was downstairs, but Henry really flinched. He squashed himself down so he was practically on the floor."

"Well, I suppose it isn't for much longer." Mum put her arm round Laura's shoulders. "I'm sorry, Laura, but you know what I mean. If he isn't happy in that noisy house, he'll be better off back at home, won't he?"

"Yes, you're right." Laura's head drooped.

"Listen –" Mum hugged her tighter – "I don't think we could now, not when it's summer and I'm working so much, but maybe later in the year…"

Laura looked at her, confused, and Mum laughed. "What I'm trying to say is – would you like us to get a dog of our own?"

Laura gasped, making Henry blink and look up at her. "Really?"

"Mm-hm. We could go to the shelter over in Linmere. I know they have lots of dogs looking for homes – maybe not puppies as cute as Henry, but I'm sure they're still gorgeous. I could look after a dog while you're at school. When I'm cleaning one of the cottages, it could come and play in the garden. I'm sure that would be all right."

Laura nodded slowly. "I'd love to have our own dog." She looked down at Henry's silky head, flopped over her lap, and let out a little sigh, although she did her best to hide it from Mum.

She ought to be so happy and she was, she really was.

But it was so hard to think of loving another dog as much as she loved Henry.

# Chapter Six

"I really love walking him," Laura
told Annie, as they wandered along
the beach together. Laura had popped
over to see if Henry wanted a walk,
and Annie had said she'd come, too.
"It's been so nice of you to let me," she
added.

Henry was darting over the damp
sand at the edge of the sea, making

squeaky yapping noises at the waves.
"I took him down to the village with
me yesterday, and everybody we met
stopped and patted him. He had a fan
club outside the sweet shop," Laura
said, giggling as Henry glared fiercely
at a pile of seaweed.

"I wish Molly and the others liked
him as much you do," said Annie. "She
still hasn't forgiven him for chewing
up her bag." Then she sighed. "I'm not
sure what's going to happen when I go
off to uni, either. Mum and Dad said
I could have a present for finishing
my exams, and I'd wanted a puppy for
so long… Mum said she'll look after
him, but she isn't really a dog person.
I hope he's going to be OK." She gave
her shoulders a little shake and smiled

at Laura. "I'm
sure he will
be, don't look
so worried!
Anyway,
Laura, why
don't you
have a dog?
You're brilliant
with Henry! Is it that
your mum's too busy?"

"Actually, she just said we could get
a dog from the rescue centre! And
it's all because of Henry. She said she
could see how much I love him, and
that maybe I should have a dog of my
own." Laura didn't say that she and her
mum thought they'd be better dog-
owners than Annie, but she was sure

it was true. How could Annie have asked for a puppy just a few months before she went away to university?

Annie nodded, looking thoughtful. "Your mum's right," she murmured. "Sorry, but we'd better head back now, Laura. I said I'd go to the shops for some crisps and things – we're having a party for Zara's birthday tonight."

Henry darted behind the sofa with his tail tucked between his legs. He wasn't sure what was going on. He'd been sleeping in his basket in the kitchen when Logan had tripped over it and nearly trodden on him. Logan had just groaned and laughed, and then

shoved the basket into the utility room.
Henry had decided to get out of the
way, but somehow the living room was
even busier than the kitchen. Everyone
seemed to be stomping around, and
the music was so loud it felt like the
house was shaking.

He peered round the arm of the
sofa and whined, looking for Annie.
He couldn't see her anywhere.
Uncertainly, he scurried along the
edge of the room, making for the
open door that led out to the garden.
He could smell the fresh air and the
sharp, salty tang of the sea. Perhaps
Annie was outside? Or maybe he'd
find Laura – he was sure her house was
somewhere nearby. He could curl up
and snuggle with her on her bed again.

That would be a much better place to sleep.

Henry nosed his way out into the dark garden…

"Laura? Are you awake, sweetheart?"

Laura sat up in bed. She was half awake. She'd been dreaming, and everything still felt strange and dreamlike now. The thudding sound of the music from her dream was still there. She shook her head, trying to shake it away, but it didn't help.

Laura blinked and rubbed her eyes, realizing at last that the music was real. And loud!

"What's going on?"

"The people from the farmhouse, again," Mum sighed. "I'm going to have to go and get them to turn the music off. It's one o'clock in the morning, for goodness' sake! I thought I'd better wake you up and tell you. I'll be back soon though, OK?"

Laura nodded and peered out of her window. The farmhouse was all lit up and she could see the shadows of people dancing against the curtains. The music was so loud her window seemed to be shaking.

"Henry!" Laura gasped, suddenly imagining the little dog shut in the house with all that noise. He must be terrified. She leaped out of bed, shoving her feet into her slippers and grabbing a hoody. Then she hurried down the stairs. Mum hadn't locked the front door, so Laura could just slip out behind her.

"What are you doing?" her mum asked, jumping as Laura touched her sleeve. "You gave me a fright, Laura. I didn't even hear you coming up behind me." She rolled her eyes. "I suppose that isn't a surprise, is it?"

"I just remembered about Henry," Laura explained. "I'm worried about him, Mum."

"Oh dear, I hadn't thought of that. Poor little dog!" Mum knocked on the door, and Laura stood next to her, huddled into her hoody. She hoped that Annie and her friends weren't going to be annoyed about being asked to turn off the music.

The yard looked so different in the dark, full of odd shadows and strange shapes. Laura caught her breath, her heart suddenly thumping as one of the shadows moved – and came slinking towards them. She grabbed her mum's arm with a squeak.

"What is it? Oh, honestly, are they never going to answer this door?"

"Mum, there's something…" The shadow settled into a little brown and white shape, padding across the yard. "Oh! Oh, Henry, it's you!" Laura gave a shaky laugh. For about half a second, she really had wondered if it was a ghost!

"Henry?" Mum turned round to look. "He's out here on his own?" Shaking her head crossly, she banged on the door again.

Laura scooped Henry up in her arms, hugging him tight. He licked her cheek and snuggled his head under her chin. "Did you slip out? Was it too noisy for you, too? Poor puppy! I wish I could just take you back to the cottage with me. I'd look after you."

She perched on the bench outside the farmhouse, loving the feel of the puppy in her arms, squirmy and soft. "I bet they haven't even noticed you've gone," she whispered in Henry's fluffy ear.

Then she sat up straighter, suddenly getting an idea. "Mum… Couldn't we just take Henry back home with us for the rest of the night? He's scared of the noise."

Mum shook her head sadly. "I wish we could, Laura. But don't worry, I'm going to make them turn the music down. Oh, at last!"

Someone had finally opened the door. One of the boys was standing there, peering out as though he was surprised to see Laura's mum. It was Logan, the one she'd seen taking Henry out that first day, Laura realized.

"Yes?" he said sullenly.

"Can you please turn that music off! Do you know what time it is?"

Laura's mum sounded really annoyed.

*If it had been me*, Laura thought, *I would have done as I was told straight away*. That was the kind of voice Mum used when she was sending Laura to her room. But Logan didn't seem to care. He just kept saying that it wasn't all that late. Laura could tell that her mum was getting crosser by the second, and she could feel Henry tensing up in her arms.

94

"Come on," she muttered. "I'll have to take you back in a minute, but not till it's all sorted out. It isn't fair." She hurried round the corner of the farmhouse, where the angry voices weren't so clear, and stood there stroking Henry and murmuring to him.

"Oh!" The music went off, and the sudden silence was eerie. It sounded almost louder than the music had, and the night seemed darker all at once. Laura felt Henry wriggle in her arms. "I know, I suppose we ought to go back. I expect Mum's told them about you, too, by now." Reluctantly, Laura padded round the corner of the house.

"There you are!" Her mum sounded relieved.

"Sorry – Henry was scared." Laura came up to the door and looked at Logan. Several other people were behind him now, and Laura wished she'd stayed to support her mum. It must have been really hard having to tell them all what to do. None of them looked very happy.

Laura peered round Mum's shoulder. Annie didn't seem to be there, but she could see Annie's friend Molly.

Laura was just about to ask where Annie was, so she could give Henry back, when Molly stepped forward. "How did he get out here?" she asked. "I bet someone left that gate open again."

"We found him in the yard. He doesn't like loud noises and shouting…" Laura whispered, holding him out to Molly.

Molly
grabbed him,
but Henry
wriggled and
twisted, and
Molly squealed
and let go. He
landed heavily on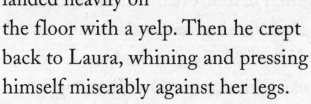
the floor with a yelp. Then he crept
back to Laura, whining and pressing
himself miserably against her legs.

Laura was gentle and friendly,
and her house was quiet. She played
with him, and took him for walks,
and didn't yank his lead to hurry him
up. Even when he was scared, like
tonight, Laura always protected him.
He slunk round behind Laura's fluffy
slippers and barked at the other girl.

He barked as loud as he could, but it came out as a shrill, frightened noise.

"Oh, stop it, you silly dog. Come here," Molly said, leaning down to grab him again.

Henry snapped his teeth at her crossly, just grazing the back of her hand. He didn't really mean to bite, but everything was just so scary.

"Hey!" Molly snatched her hand away with a gasp. "Ow! Bad dog!"

Henry heard Laura protest, but Molly picked him up again and marched into the house. Henry peered over her arm, scrabbling and whining and looking for Laura. He could still see her, leaning against her mum and crying. He clawed at the girl's sleeve, trying to wriggle free, but this time he couldn't get away.

"Naughty dog! No biting!" Molly said, carrying him into the utility room and dumping him down on the tiles. "Just stay there!"

She slammed the door, and Henry crouched in front of it, shaking all over. He was all alone and so frightened.

Whimpering, he turned round and slunk across the floor to his basket. He climbed in, pressing his head against the soft side and burrowing half under the crumpled blanket. He wanted to hide himself away from everything.

# Chapter Seven

"Are they really going to go home? Even though they're supposed to stay nearly another week?" Laura stared at her mum. She felt like crying.

"They have to," Mum said with a sigh. "I spoke to Jenny from the letting agency this morning, after I'd already had three different families complaining to me about the noise.

She says she'll call them and explain that they've got to leave."

"Today?" Laura asked, her voice very small.

"I think so. Sorry, sweetheart." Mum hugged her. "But I expect Henry will be happy to go home. He hasn't liked being in a house full of people."

"We don't know what his home's like," Laura muttered into her mum's sleeve. "Maybe that's full of people, too. Annie might have loads of brothers and sisters." She couldn't help being down. She felt too miserable to look on the bright side. Her mum just hugged her tighter. She could tell how upset Laura was.

"Do you think I'll be able to say goodbye to him?" Laura said, her voice still muffled, so that her mum had to tilt her head to listen.

"I hope so. I'll have to go over to pick up the keys and make sure they've left the house nice and tidy. You can come with me, if you like. Although no one's going to be in a very good mood," she warned.

Laura looked up and nodded, biting her lip. She didn't really want to listen to another argument like the night before, but she couldn't miss the chance to say goodbye.

"I'm glad you won't have to have everybody complaining to you any more," she said, resting her head against her mum's shoulder.

"Me, too. And, Laura, I really did mean it about us getting a dog. You've been so good at helping with Henry. Very responsible. Try and think of the positive things, OK?"

Laura nodded. She was trying. But all she could think of was Henry last night, whimpering as Molly carried him away.

Henry was sitting underneath the coffee table. He didn't really want to be there, but he didn't know where else to go. He'd been curled up on Annie's lap, enjoying being cuddled and fussed over, when the sharp sound of the doorbell had made him jump. And it had made everyone start shouting again. Annie had got up, leaving him on the sofa, but there was just too much noise to stay there. So he'd clambered down into the small, safe space under the table.

Perhaps he should go and sit in his basket? If he went to sleep for a while, maybe everything would quieten down again. Henry poked his nose out from under the table and then flinched back as a suitcase on wheels went rattling by. But then he shook himself briskly and went trotting out after the case. He wasn't going to sleep. He would go and find Laura, instead. They could go for a walk. Or even just

snuggle up together, the way they had
the other day.

Both of the times when he'd got out
of the house before, he'd slipped out
of the side gate in the garden, so he
went that way again, keeping close to
the walls and skittering past the piles
of bags and beach stuff. Whenever
he heard people come hurrying past,
Henry froze. But no one seemed to
notice him, anyway. The back door
that led into the little garden was open,
like it had been the night before, and
Henry slipped out. His feathery tail
started to wag delightedly to and fro.
He would see Laura soon!

But the garden gate was closed.
Henry sat in front of it, confused, his
tail sweeping from side to side on the

dusty path. He had only ever seen it open. This wasn't right. After a minute or so, it was clear that the gate wasn't going to move. He got up and sniffed at it, and then stood up on his hind paws and scrabbled away, but all it did was creak a little and rattle. It stayed very firmly shut.

Henry gave the gate one last hopeful look. Then he sniffed at the tall plants growing up beside the fence and peered between the slats. There was the path. That was the way Laura had always taken him. That path would take him back to her, he was sure.

Henry crept along the base of the fence, pushing his way through the thick stems and scratching half-heartedly at the wooden posts here and there. But the fence was solid, and the wooden slats were too close together even for a little dog to squeeze through. Henry slumped down under a clump of poppies, feeling helpless. His coat was tangled, and full of grass seeds and bits of twig. He was hot and cross – and he was still stuck. He sank his chin down on his paws and gazed miserably at the ground. Then his nose twitched thoughtfully.

Right in front of him, there was a small dip under the fence. It had started as nothing more than a puddle of rain dripping down from a bush, but the water had smoothed the earth away, and now there was a definite hollow. Almost big enough for a little dog to squirm through.

Henry sprang up with an excited whine, and began to scrape and scuff with his soft puppy claws at the dry earth. It only took a few minutes to widen the hole out and dig it a little deeper, and then deeper still... Until it was just big enough for him

to force his
head under.
He squeezed
and wriggled
and shoved until
he was outside on
the path.

Henry stared around triumphantly
and shook the dusty earth out of his
fur. Then he set off, his head held high,
to find Laura.

Laura stood next to her mum – as
close as she could. Laura wanted Mum
to know that she was right there beside
her. Logan was telling Mum that it
was completely unfair they were being

made to leave. Laura thought it wasn't fair that her mum just had to stand there and listen to people shouting at her again.

"Look, I can see that you're upset, but the best thing to do is to send an email to the letting agency," Mum said patiently.

Laura peered round Mum, trying to see into the other rooms. She wasn't sure where Henry was. She could see his basket in the utility room, but he wasn't in it. Maybe he was hiding somewhere, because of all the angry voices?

"I just need to check round the house to make sure that everything's tidy," Mum explained. "It looks like you're mostly packed up. Are you bringing the cars round to the front? You can put them in the yard for loading up, if you like."

Laura trailed after Mum round the upstairs rooms. The group were really going, any minute now. If she didn't find Henry soon, she wouldn't be able to say goodbye to him at all. Maybe Annie had taken him for a last walk, she thought sadly.

But then she saw Annie packing up stuff from one of the bathrooms. So that wasn't it. Wherever could he be? She longed to ask, but Annie looked unhappy about leaving, too, and Laura didn't want to make things any harder for Mum. She'd see Henry in a minute, as they were putting him in the car. Even if it was just for one last quick cuddle.

# Chapter Eight

Henry peered round the corner of the farmhouse, eyeing the commotion going on in the yard. He wanted to see if he could find Laura, but a car had driven up, and then another one, both braking sharply and sending up a spray of gravel and dust.

A car door slammed and he flinched back. Maybe he wouldn't go this way.

Henry looked around nervously.
Perhaps Laura was at the beach? But
he wasn't sure he wanted to go further
down the clifftop path by himself.
Instead, he pattered a little way across
the gravel and crept in between two
large pots of flowers.

He'd sit here and watch
for Laura.
And then,
there she was!
Coming out of the
farmhouse – she had
been there all the time!
Henry yelped and
poked out his nose from
between the flowerpots. But then
a car door slammed again and there
were people everywhere, flinging bags

into the cars and shouting to each
other. He didn't dare go past them.
Henry wriggled back, deeper into the
little damp space between the pots.
The trailing leaves hid him and he
felt quite safe, but he couldn't reach
Laura…

Laura stood with her mum by the
front door of the farmhouse, looking
at the two cars. Neither of them had
space for a proper travel crate for a
dog, she noticed. She couldn't even
see any room for Henry to sit. If they
put him in the boot with all those
bags, one of them could easily topple
over and squash him.

"Mum," she said, tugging at her mum's sleeve. "I still haven't seen Henry. He wasn't in the house."

Her mum glanced down at her. "Wasn't he? I suppose I didn't see him, either…"

Just then, Annie came hurrying out of the front door, her face pale under her tan. "Has anyone seen Henry?" she asked. "I still can't find him and I've been looking for ages!"

"I thought he was shut in the utility room," Logan called back. "You said you wanted to keep him out of the way while we were packing."

"Yes, I know. But he isn't there now," Annie said. "The front door's wide open. And so's the back one."

Laura glanced worriedly at her

mum. Maybe Henry had gone down to the beach on his own. He could be *anywhere*.

"Yeah, but the garden gate's shut, isn't it?" Molly straightened up, frowning. She'd been shoving bags into one of the cars and now she pushed her hair out of her eyes, looking grumpy and hot. "He escaped that way the other times, so we've all been really careful about keeping it closed today."

"Then where is he?" Annie wailed. "He's not in the house. I've checked everywhere, under all the beds. I even went through all the cupboards. He must have got out."

Logan closed the boot of the car with a thump – it only just shut, the car was so packed.

"Not even sure we can fit him in the car," he called to Annie. "Maybe you should just leave him behind."

Laura stared at him in horror. She thought he must be joking – surely he had to be? But he wasn't smiling.

She clenched her fists, suddenly furious. How dare he?

"You can't just leave Henry behind. It's because of people like you that there are shelters full of abandoned dogs!" Laura yelled at him. "How can you say that? You don't even know where he is! He could be lost on the cliff, or down on the beach." Then she drew back against her mum, feeling her cheeks redden.

Logan shrugged, but he looked embarrassed, too. "I didn't actually mean we'd leave him…" he muttered.

"Of course I'm not leaving him!" Annie gulped. It seemed as though she was about to cry. "Laura, do you really think he could have gone all the way down to the beach?"

Laura nodded. "He loves it there."

"Well, don't be too long." Logan folded his arms, leaning against the car.

"I'll come and help look." Laura started to follow Annie, then glanced back at her mum to check it was OK.

"Yes, you'd better," her mum said. "I'll come, too, once I've got the keys."

Laura followed Annie along the front of the house, to the corner where the path started. She was trying to think of all the places Henry might be. Where had he specially liked when they'd been out on walks? Maybe he was digging around in one of those piles of smelly seaweed on the beach again.

Then something made her glance sideways, down at the flowerpots. Perhaps it was a tiny whimper, or perhaps a scuffling of puppy claws.

He was there – gazing out at her. Laura could see his tail, wagging just a little, as though he wasn't quite sure whether to be happy. He didn't want to come out, she guessed. Too much shouting and banging and general horribleness.

Laura stopped. She'd have to tell Annie, of course. Only … if she didn't, maybe they would go without him, like Logan had said. Maybe they'd leave Henry, and she could keep him… Laura dug her fingernails into her palms, hesitating.

But she couldn't say nothing, even though she wanted to, so much.

Laura took a deep breath and called after Annie, who was just disappearing round the corner of the house. "He's here!"

"Henry!" Annie came dashing over, her footsteps crunching on the gravel. But the puppy edged backwards, further into the space between the pots.

"I think he's scared," Laura said sadly. She glanced round and saw that Mum had hurried up beside her. She looked sad, too.

"Come on, Henry," Annie called.

"Can't you just grab him?" Logan yelled.

Annie turned round to glare at him. "Shut up, Logan! He doesn't like people shouting – you're making it worse. Come on, Henry…"

Laura kneeled down in front of the pots and looked in at the puppy. "Henry," she whisper-called. "It's OK. Come on out."

Henry eyed her and then glanced at Annie. Very slowly, he started to creep towards them, paw by paw, as though he wasn't sure if he was doing the right thing. He then made a sudden little rush and jumped at Laura, scrambling on to her lap. He was shivering and Laura wrapped her arms around him.

She stood up slowly and rubbed her cheek against his soft fur one last time. Then, reluctantly, she held him out to Annie.

Annie looked at her for a moment. At last she shook her head. "No..." she said quietly. "No. I think you'd better keep him. You'll look after him a lot better than I have."

"W-what?" Laura stammered. She'd

wished and wished for Annie to say just that. Now she thought she might have imagined it.

"Keep him. He can be yours, if you like."

"Hang on…" Laura's mum shook her head. "That's really nice of you, but he must have been an expensive puppy. I don't think we can take him."

"Oh, Mum!" Laura gasped, her eyes filling with tears. "Please…" She'd been so happy, just for a second.

But Annie smiled – a stiff, unhappy sort of smile. "I shouldn't ever have asked for him, it was really selfish. He'll be much happier with you." She sighed and put out her hand to stroke Henry's soft ears. "I'll miss you," she murmured.

"Well…" Laura's mum frowned. "I suppose, if you're sure."

"So, I can keep him?" Laura asked, in a whisper.

Mum nodded. "Yes!"

Annie turned away sharply, and grabbed Henry's basket and bowls and food out of the car. She pushed them into Mum's arms and then dived into the front seat as though she wanted to get away as quickly as possible.

Laura stood watching as the cars backed slowly out of the yard. Henry was still in her arms – they were going, really going, and leaving Henry behind with her. She stared down at him anxiously. Would he be upset, seeing Annie leave? But he looked quite happy snuggled up against her T-shirt.

"I've got a dog!" she said to Mum, only half believing it. Was this all just some kind of dream?

"You have!" Mum agreed, her eyes wide. "Oh my goodness! We've got a dog…" She glanced at the basket and bowls and bag of food she was holding, and shook her head slightly. "I suppose we'd better go and put these inside."

As Laura followed her mum back into the house, Henry licked her ear, making her giggle. She couldn't be dreaming, if her ear was all wet… She stood in the hall with Henry, kicking off her flip-flops, and watched Mum hang the puppy's red lead on one of the coat hooks.

"It looks perfect," Laura whispered in Henry's ear. "It looks just like you belong!"

# Monty the Sad Puppy

For everyone who asked for another Labrador book!

# Chapter One

"Shall we head down to the field now?"
Amelie suggested. "Then we can give
Monty a really good run." She laughed.
"Look, he heard me!"

Monty's soft black ears had
suddenly pricked up and he was
staring hopefully at Amelie. He was
only a puppy but he already had long
Labrador legs and he loved to run.

Her brother checked the time on his phone. "Yeah, OK, but not for too long. We've already been out twenty minutes and he's only supposed to walk for about twenty-five."

Amelie sighed. "I know the leaflet said that but look at him, Josh! He's desperate! He wants a proper run, don't you, Monty?"

The little black Labrador frisked round her feet with an excited bark. "It's just not fair, is it? You love walks so much and so do we!"

Amelie crouched down to rub his head and run his ears through her fingers. His ears were so silky, and she loved the way he closed his eyes and stuck his nose in the air every time she did it.

"Well, it won't be that long till he
can go on really big walks," Josh said
and then grinned. "He's already five
months old – so that's only another
seven months to go!"

Amelie rolled her eyes. Josh thought
he was so funny sometimes – she and
Mum reckoned it was a teenage boy
thing. "Come on, Josh, pleeease? If we

go to the field then we can take the alley and go the quick way home."

When they'd first got Monty, three months earlier, the breeder had given them a leaflet of tips on how to look after a Labrador puppy properly. She'd explained that Monty couldn't go out for walks at all till he'd had his vaccinations. And even then, they'd have to be careful not to overwalk him while he was still under a year. The information leaflet suggested a five-minute rule – only five minutes of proper exercise for every month of Monty's age, so as not to injure his growing legs.

Amelie knew it was the right thing to do but she still didn't like it. Their walks seemed to have hardly got going before they had to turn round again.

"I suppose…" Josh agreed. "At least he'll be nice and hungry for his dinner. Come on then, Monty! Let's go to the field!"

Monty pranced along happily. He loved going out in the afternoons with Amelie and Josh. In the morning he went out with their dad, who did too much stopping to chat to people while he walked round the lake. Amelie and Josh raced about and threw sticks, and they usually brought toys for him to chase. He pulled eagerly at his lead, making for the gate out to the field.

"Heel, Monty," Amelie said, pulling him back gently. She and Josh had been taking Monty to puppy training classes, and they'd been told not to let him pull when they were walking to heel.

Monty dropped back obediently and Josh fumbled a treat out of his pocket. "Good dog!"

"You wouldn't think he'd only been going to training for three weeks, would you?" Amelie said proudly, as she opened the gate.

Josh grinned. "He's a greedy pig. He'll do anything for those treats."

"Yes, but some dogs never learn to do things like that. I mean, what about Maisy? Grandad can't ever get her to sit and stay, and she only walks to heel when she feels like it. Think about last week!"

"Yeah…" Josh shook his head, remembering. Grandad had come with them on a walk to the park with

Maisy, his little dachsund. They'd
walked past a girl eating a biscuit
and Maisy had nibbled it right out of
her hand. Her mum had been really
cross, even though Grandad had
said sorry loads of times. He had felt
awful about it but Maisy hadn't been
bothered at all...

"I reckon that's because she's a
dachshund, though," Josh pointed
out. "They're not very easy to train.
Labradors like Monty are good at this
sort of thing. I mean, you don't ever
get dachshund Guide Dogs, do you?"

Amelie giggled. "Maisy would be a
useless Guide Dog. Maybe you're right
about all Labs being good but I do
think Monty's extra-clever. Here, you
can take his lead for a bit, if you like."

Monty was staring up at them both hopefully, waiting for the chance to dash off into the field. Amelie patted his head, then passed the lead to Josh.

"Come on, Monty," she called, jogging backwards on to the long grass around the edge of the football pitch.

Amelie loved Newland Park. She remembered going there when she was tiny. Dad had taken her for walks round the lake almost every day and let her throw food to the ducks. But it was only now they had a dog that she realized how lucky they were to have the park so close by. All the houses in their street backed on to it.

Josh and Monty raced past Amelie, Monty barking and yipping with excitement. She ran after them and then stopped to look through the wire fence as she reached their back garden. Sometimes Dad came out to drink a cup of tea if he was having a break from work. She peered past the apple tree, trying to see further up the garden, but he wasn't there. She waved, just in case, before chasing after her brother and Monty. The puppy was so excited that he was dashing around in circles.

"Watch out, Josh!" Amelie cried but it was too late.

Monty had seen Amelie coming and decided to race towards her, pulling the lead tight around Josh's legs and yanking his feet out from under him. Her tall, skinny brother fell like a tree, collapsing into the long grass with a groan.

"Catch him!" he called. "Amelie! The lead!"

"I've got it!" Amelie yelled, snatching at Monty's trailing lead as he danced around her. "Here, Monty. You silly dog," she said lovingly. "What did you think you were doing, hmm?"

"I'm fine, thank you for asking," Josh muttered, heaving himself up out of the grass. "Uuurgh. I think I landed in something disgusting."

Amelie peered at the brown patch down the side of Josh's jeans. "It's only mud," she said reassuringly. "You are OK, aren't you?"

"Yes." Josh sighed. "No thanks to you, Monty. Well, I'll know not to let him wind me up in the lead like that again. I wouldn't have thought he was that strong!"

Monty sat at Amelie's feet, gazing

up at them both and panting happily.
He had no idea what Josh was talking
about but he was hoping it didn't mean
the end of the walk.

Amelie had thought Josh would be
able to sneak upstairs and change
before Dad spotted him when they got
home. But their dad was in the hallway
when they returned – and so was
Mum, which was really unusual. She
was hardly ever home early from the
shop where she worked.

Amelie unclipped Monty's lead and
he dashed off to the kitchen for a drink
of water. Mum gave Amelie a hug but
Amelie looked up at her anxiously –

she had a serious expression on her face.

"What's wrong?" Josh asked, forgetting about his jeans.

Mum took a deep breath. "It's Grandad..." she started and Amelie's stomach clenched. Their mum's dad hadn't been well for a while. A few months ago he'd had a stroke and been in hospital for a few days. But Amelie thought he'd been getting better now he was back at home again. He'd seemed fine when they'd last seen him.

"What's happened?" she whispered, her eyes suddenly hot with tears.

Mum put an arm round her shoulders. "It's another stroke. Don't panic, Amelie, it looks like he'll be all right. But it's going to take longer for him to recover this time. He's probably not going to be able to look after himself at home, even once he's allowed out of hospital. He'll need to be in a nursing home for a bit, where there are staff who can help."

"Oh…" Amelie leaned against her, relieved. For a moment she'd thought Mum was going to give them much worse news. "Poor Grandad," she said.

Josh frowned. "Do you mean he'll always need to be looked after, Mum?"

"We're not sure." Mum and Dad exchanged a worried look. "It's only just happened, Josh. I haven't even been to see him yet. But from what the hospital said, it's more serious this time. Grandad will probably have to move permanently to some sort of sheltered housing. Somewhere there's lot of support."

"What's going to happen to Maisy?" Amelie asked, looking up. "Will Grandad be able to take her with him?"

Mum stared at her. "Oh my goodness. I'd forgotten about Maisy. Grandad's neighbours fed her the last time he was in hospital."

Dad ran his hand through his hair. "That's not going to work this time, though. She's going to need a proper home." He looked thoughtfully round the hallway, as though he was imagining another dog trotting down it. Amelie caught her breath.

"Your mum and I talked about this a while ago," Dad went on. "After all, Maisy already knows us, doesn't she?"

Mum nodded. "We mentioned it to Grandad, too. That Maisy could come and live here with us."

Monty wandered back into the hallway, looking curiously at them all still standing there. Amelie crouched down to stroke him and he nuzzled against her, licking her cheek. Amelie thought maybe he could taste that she'd been crying. His tail was waving, just a little, the way it did when he was worried.

"Oh, Monty…" Amelie murmured. "How would you feel about sharing your home with another dog?"

# Chapter Two

"So you're going to have two dogs?" Ella asked, leaning across the table to whisper. "You're so lucky, Amelie, I don't even have one! Is Maisy cute?"

Amelie nodded. "She's a gorgeous colour – russet, Grandad calls her, and her coat's so glossy, even shinier than Monty's. She's tiny but she thinks she's in charge. She's always bossing my grandad around!" Then she sighed. "He's going to miss her so much – I mean, he's had Maisy for eight years. I'm really excited about looking after her and it's going to be great for Monty, having a friend at home all the time. But I wish Maisy could stay with Grandad."

"I'm sorry he's in hospital, Amelie," Ella said. "But I bet he's happy you'll be looking after Maisy."

"Mum told Grandad we'd go and get her today. Dad's going to pick me up from school in the car, then we'll go straight over to the house."

"Are you two actually discussing the Romans?" Miss Garrett asked, leaning over Amelie's shoulder and making her jump.

"Um. We were…" she muttered. "Sorry, Miss Garrett."

"Sorry, Miss Garrett," Ella repeated.

"Well, get on with it, girls. I'd like a plan drawn up by break time, please."

Ella sighed as their teacher moved on to the next table. "I wish we didn't always have to make things for topic work. My Viking ship last year was just embarrassing."

"What do you think you'll do this time?" Amelie asked. "What about a costume? You could make a Roman dress, if your mum wouldn't mind you using an old sheet." She flicked through the book they'd found in the school library. "Oh, wow… I'd like to make something like that!"

Ella peered at the mosaic picture of

a fierce-looking guard dog. "All those tiny squares! It'll take hours."

"It looks really fun. I could cut the squares out of craft foam."

Ella nodded. "I suppose so. Don't forget you're going to have two dogs to play with, though!"

Amelie nodded. "I haven't – I can't wait for this afternoon!"

Amelie picked up the dog carrier and walked carefully out to the car, murmuring soothingly to Maisy. She told the little dachshund how excited Monty would be when she arrived and how much fun they were all going to have.

Maisy had been really pleased to see them when they arrived at Grandad's house. Amelie thought she'd probably had a lonely sort of day, since she was used to having Grandad around most of the time. But she hadn't been keen on going in her carrier at all. She'd backed away from Amelie, her long ears shaking.

"Maybe she thinks we're taking

her to the vet," Dad suggested, as he unlocked the car.

"Shh, Dad! You know Grandad says she understands that word! You have to spell it out," Amelie reminded him.

"Oh, yes. Sorry, Maisy. Are you OK with the carrier on your lap, Amelie? Hold it tight."

Amelie wrapped her arms firmly around the carrier. There was no sound at all from inside but she could see Maisy through the holes in the plastic sides. The dachshund was standing up with her nose pressed against the wire door.

"Sit down, Maisy-dog," Amelie whispered, as Dad started the car. "You'll wobble." But Maisy stayed on her feet, even though the movement of the car made her lurch about. Amelie kept on whispering encouraging things but Maisy seemed too confused to sit down. She just kept on slipping from side to side, her little black claws scrabbling against the plastic floor of the carrier. The blanket Grandad kept in there was all scrunched up at the back. Maisy wasn't whining or yapping, which was really odd. Grandad always said she was the chattiest dog he'd ever met but now she was completely silent.

"Is she all right?" Dad asked, as they stopped at the lights.

"I don't know…" Amelie admitted.

"She looks really nervous. Maybe you're right and she does think she's going to the V–E–T."

Dad glanced over at the carrier, frowning. "We're nearly home. Not long now, Maisy."

Amelie stood on the doorstep, waiting for Dad to find his keys and looking at the hunched little dog inside the carrier. She wouldn't have minded so much if Maisy had howled all the way home. Amelie hurried into the house and put the carrier down in the hallway, just as Josh came out of the kitchen holding a half-eaten piece of toast. Monty raced after him, whining

with excitement as he saw Amelie
and Dad. Then he saw the carrier and
skidded to a halt.

There was a skittering, scrabbling
noise from inside and a low growl.
Monty retreated behind Josh, his tail
drooping. Amelie looked anxiously
between the two dogs. Dad had said
that they ought to introduce Maisy and
Monty to each other slowly but Amelie
hadn't thought it would be a problem.
Monty had been to Grandad's house
and Maisy had been coming to their
house for years. Why wouldn't they
be happy to see each other? Maybe it
just wasn't the same without Grandad
there, too.

"Shall we let Maisy out now?" she
asked Dad.

Dad sighed. "Yes, I suppose we'd better. Let's keep her in the kitchen to start with. Josh, can you put Monty out in the garden? Let's give Maisy a bit of space."

"Uh-huh." Josh caught Monty's collar. The puppy was still staring at the carrier, looking confused. "Come on, Monty. Is Maisy OK? She's very quiet."

"She looks miserable," Amelie said. "Do you think she knows Grandad's ill?"

"I'm sure she knows *something*'s wrong…" Dad said. "Dogs are very good at sensing that sort of thing."

Monty peered round Josh's arm as Amelie picked up the carrier. What was going on? There was another dog in there, he could smell her. It was Maisy – he knew her. What was

Maisy doing in his house? And now Amelie was putting the carrier down in the kitchen, where his basket and his food bowl were.

He wriggled and pulled as Josh tried to unlock the back door, twisting and scrabbling so that Josh let go of him. Monty backed away clumsily, skidding on the tiles, and padded up to the carrier, sniffing hard. He stretched out one careful paw to the wire door, turning his head from side to side as he tried to work out what was going on.

There was a sharp yap from inside and Monty jumped back, tucking his tail between his legs. Then he crept forward, sniffing again. Maisy had always been friendly before. Monty's tail twitched slowly to and fro as he stared at her, confused.

"It's OK, Monty," Amelie said, gently pushing him away. "Josh's just taking you out so you don't upset Maisy, that's all."

"Come on, Monty." Josh took hold of the puppy's collar again and Monty squirmed, pulling away anxiously. Was he in trouble? This time Josh had a better grip and Monty couldn't get free. Josh let go of him outside the door and then ducked smartly back into the kitchen. Monty scampered after him but the door clicked closed just in front of his nose. Then he heard the sound of the dog flap locking, too. Josh had shut him out.

Monty stood staring at the door, his ears flattened back. Why was he stuck outside, while Maisy was in *his* kitchen?

Monty pawed at the door, whining. He wanted Amelie. He was getting hungry, too, but mostly he wanted Amelie to hold him and pat him, so he knew that everything was all right. Instead he was shut out in the garden. It felt as though he'd been there for ages.

He skittered back as the door opened suddenly and Amelie appeared. He whined – he'd been so desperate to get back in but now he wasn't sure what to do. He could smell Maisy inside – she was still there.

"Are you going to come in?" Amelie coaxed. "Come and see Maisy."

Monty looked past her into the doorway and spotted Maisy. She was sitting under the kitchen table, her head drooping. He looked up at Amelie, still unsure what was going on.

"It's just Maisy," Dad said, crouching down beside Monty. "You know Maisy." He glanced at Amelie and Josh. "This is a bit harder than I thought it would be. Let's feed them both – that should cheer them up."

Dad brought out Maisy's food and water bowls, and the big bag of dry food that Grandad used. It was the same kind that they gave Monty, Amelie noticed, except that it was for an older dog, not a puppy.

"Should we put their bowls close together?" Amelie asked. "Would that help?"

Dad shook his head. "Not yet. Let's work up to it. We'll put Maisy's over here, by the door."

Monty was looking happier now, wagging his tail eagerly as he saw his bag of food come out. But Maisy hadn't moved. She was still under the table and she wasn't paying any attention to the food Dad was pouring into her bowl. Amelie watched as

Monty wolfed down his dinner and Maisy ignored hers completely.

"I suppose she doesn't feel like eating," Josh said slowly, crouching down by the table and reaching out his hand for Maisy to sniff. But Maisy turned her head away. "She's missing him, isn't she? She knows things aren't right."

"I really hope she cheers up soon," Amelie said. "What are we going to tell Grandad?"

Dad sighed. "I'm sure she'll settle down. We can't expect her to be happy straight away."

"I guess so," Amelie said. But she hadn't thought it would be like this. She'd imagined walks and cuddles with two gorgeous dogs. Instead she had a confused puppy and a miserable dog who wouldn't even eat.

# Chapter Three

"It's all right, Monty." Amelie smoothed his ears gently. "It's going to be OK. I hope..." she added in a whisper.

She and Monty were sitting in the hallway on the bottom step. The two dogs didn't seem to be getting on very well. When they'd met before it had mostly been for walks – Amelie,

Josh and Grandad had loved going out together with the dogs. Somehow it was different now that they were sharing a house. Monty had gone up and tried to give Maisy a friendly sniff but she'd growled at him, showing her teeth, and he'd backed away, looking frightened. Amelie had decided to take Monty out of the room again and give Maisy some time to settle.

"Perhaps I should have guessed this would be confusing for you, too," Amelie muttered. "I just thought Maisy would keep you company while me and Josh were at school. Dad says you're always making sad eyes at him when he's working."

Monty leaned against Amelie's knees, enjoying the fuss she was making of him. His strange, bewildered feeling eased as she rubbed his ears. He let out a long huff of breath, his eyes half-closing.

"Ready to go, Amelie?" said Mum, walking down the stairs.

"Do I have to come?" Amelie asked, staring at Monty's ears so she didn't have to look at Mum.

"Don't you want to see Grandad?" Mum sat down on the stairs behind her. "He'd love to see you. Josh wanted to come but he's got football practice. Are you worried about going to the hospital, sweetheart? I don't think it'll be scary. Grandad's doing really well."

Amelie turned to look up at her. "It isn't that. I mean, maybe a bit but mostly I don't know what to say about Maisy. Grandad's going to ask us how she is and I don't want to tell him."

Mum put a hand on Amelie's shoulder. "Grandad's not going to expect miracles, Amelie. He'll know she's going to be upset to begin with. He's really pleased we're looking after her, you know. When I went to see him last night he said he knew you'd look after her for him."

"But I'm not looking after her!" Amelie sniffed hard and then half-laughed as Monty snuggled his damp nose against her chin. "Look – Monty can tell I'm worried. Maisy's so upset, Mum. She didn't eat dinner and she's really grumpy with Monty. I think she hates being here, full stop."

Mum nodded. "Wouldn't you, though? If you'd suddenly been taken to a new place, with people you didn't really know, and you didn't understand what was happening? And you were missing your best friend? She's only been here a couple of hours, Amelie. We've just got to give her time."

Grandad looked small, Amelie decided. That was what was so weird. He was a tall man but in the hospital bed he seemed to have shrunk.

"Ignore the pyjamas, Amelie," he said as she came in, grinning at her and trying to heave himself up against the pillows. "These horrible yellow things are from the hospital. Your mum's promised to nip back over to my house and get me my own ones."

Amelie giggled. "They are a funny colour," she agreed. Grandad looked really pale and washed out – she didn't think it was just because of the pyjamas but it was easier to pretend. "Are you feeling all right?" she asked, feeling slightly awkward.

"Just tired." Grandad reached out to pat her hand and Amelie moved closer to him – she could see how hard it was for him to lift his arm. She'd been hoping that he'd be able to come out of the hospital soon but now she could see how serious things were.

"How's Maisy?" Grandad asked. "How's Monty coping with her bossing him around? Is she being a little madam?"

Amelie swallowed. "A bit…" She wished Maisy *would* be bossy. That would be better than her being so quiet and unhappy.

"She's still getting used to the move, Dad," Amelie's mum put in. "I'm sure she'll be fine soon."

Grandad nodded but he looked worried.

"It'll be OK, Grandad," Amelie found herself saying. "I promise we'll make her happy."

"I know you will, love." Grandad smiled at her. "She's in good hands."

Amelie smiled, too, but behind her back she was digging her nails into her palms. How could they make Maisy happy when she was so upset? But now she'd made a promise. And she was going to do everything she could to keep it.

"Josh! Josh, wake up!"

"Amelie..." Josh groaned and pulled the duvet up around his ears. "What's the matter?"

Amelie perched on the edge of his bed and Monty snuffled his nose under Josh's duvet.

"Eugh! Cold," Josh moaned. "Get off, Monty."

"I need to talk to you. I've hardly slept at all, thinking about it."

"About what?" Josh sat up and looked at Amelie blearily. His hair was sticking up and he still seemed half-asleep.

"I need you to help me make Maisy happy."

"What?" Josh yawned.

"I promised Grandad," Amelie explained. "I didn't mean to, it just came out. I wanted to cheer him up… I told him we'd make Maisy happy. So now we have to."

"Me?" Josh sighed.

"Both of us! What can we do? I've just been down to feed her and Monty, and she's still not eating. She had a tiny nibble of her biscuits and then went back to her basket. And I think Monty's scared of her. He kept looking over at her the whole time he was eating."

Josh ran his hands through his hair and sighed. "I wish the hospital let dogs in. She's missing Grandad and he's missing her. If only they could see each other."

Amelie nodded. "She's only little – do you think we could smuggle her in? Maybe in my school bag?"

Josh grinned. "I wish we could. But she'd bark her head off if we tried to put her in a bag. We might get banned from the hospital."

"I suppose so…" Then Amelie sat up, staring at him. "She can't *see* Grandad … but what about hearing him? We could phone him at the hospital and he can talk to Maisy!"

Josh nodded. "Yes! That's perfect, Amelie! Let's go and do it now."

Amelie jumped up but then she stopped. "I'm not sure we should, not before school. Grandad looked so tired yesterday – he might still be asleep." She sighed. "Let's call him when we get home. A few hours won't matter…" It just seemed such a long time for Maisy to wait.

Amelie spent the whole day worrying about Monty and Maisy. Dad had said that he'd try to take them both out for a morning walk but Amelie wasn't sure Maisy would want to go. She'd been out in the garden to wee but she hadn't seemed to enjoy the fresh air. She'd just trailed back into the house. When Monty wanted walks, he danced around her eagerly, or sometimes he sat in front of his lead, whining and trying to claw it off its hook. Maisy hadn't done anything like that.

"What's the matter?" Ella asked her at break time.

"Monty and Maisy aren't getting on," Amelie admitted. "I got so excited about having Maisy come to live with us, I didn't even think about what it would really be like."

Ella looked sympathetic. "But dogs do get new owners sometimes. I bet she'll get used to you soon."

"I hope so. We've got a plan, anyway." Amelie explained about the phone call and Ella nodded.

"That sounds like a great idea," she said, as the bell went. "Don't worry, Amelie. I'm sure hearing your grandad's voice will cheer Maisy up."

Amelie had promised to wait for Josh so they could phone Grandad together but he seemed to take hours to walk home from school that afternoon. She watched out for him from her bedroom window with Monty curled up on his cushion next to her.

Monty was supposed to sleep in the kitchen – he definitely preferred sleeping in Amelie's room, though. Mum and Dad had told Amelie he shouldn't sleep on her bed, because when he was fully grown there'd be no room for her. So he had a big cushion next to the bed instead.

As soon as Amelie saw her brother coming down the road, she leaped from the windowsill and galloped down the stairs. Monty had been half-asleep but he woke up as Amelie dashed past him. Where was she going? He blinked after her, confused, and then got up, shaking himself awake to follow her.

"OK, OK, I'm coming," Josh said, pulling his mobile out of his pocket as Amelie dragged him into the kitchen. The two baskets were still at opposite ends of the room – Maisy's little dachshund-sized one and the great big basket that Dad had bought for Monty to grow into.

"Dad said she wouldn't go for a walk this morning," Amelie told Josh. "She wouldn't even get out of her basket."

"Maybe this'll help," Josh said, searching for Grandad's number. Amelie crouched down next to Maisy, eyeing the little dog anxiously. She really hoped this would work.

Maisy was curled up in a ball, with one paw stretched over her muzzle – almost as if she was trying to cover her eyes. She'd obviously heard Amelie and Josh coming. She opened one dark eye and stared at them suspiciously.

"Josh! Amelie! Your mum told me about your idea!" Amelie could hear Grandad's voice, small and hollow sounding, from the phone.

"Hi, Grandad. I'm putting you on speaker – Maisy's right here."

Before Josh could even touch the screen, Maisy was on her feet, her ears as pricked as a dachshund's ever could be. Josh laughed. "Grandad, she can definitely hear you! Say hello to her!"

"Maisy! Oh, there's my lovely girl…"

Amelie blinked back sudden tears. She didn't really know why she was crying – it was just that Grandad sounded so happy to be talking to Maisy. Maisy looked happier, too. She had her nose pressed up against the phone and her tail was wagging the tiniest bit. It was working!

Amelie beamed at Josh and he grinned back at her.

Monty sat alone in the kitchen doorway, watching them fuss over Maisy, his head hanging low. As Amelie reached up to high-five Josh, he looked up eagerly, his tail starting to wag, hoping that she'd notice him. But Amelie was too busy watching Maisy.

# Chapter Four

"Come on, Monty! Walk time!"

Monty raced down the hallway, almost crashing into Amelie's legs. He was desperate for a really good long walk.

It had been five days since Grandad had gone into hospital. Josh and Amelie had done their best but walks had taken second place to hospital visits. They'd even had to miss Monty's dog-training class on Saturday. But when they went to visit Grandad on Sunday he had told them to stop fussing. "I'm definitely on the mend," he told Amelie firmly. "You need to go home and spend some time with those dogs. Sunday afternoon's the perfect time for a long walk."

Monty ducked back as Maisy suddenly appeared from behind Amelie's feet. He was still nervous around her. Maisy didn't seem to care that she was so much smaller than he was. If he came near her food or her basket, she'd bare her teeth at him and growl. So Maisy was coming on the walk, too? He dropped back, crouching low and wagging his tail a little to try and show her that he was friendly.

"It's OK, Monty. Come on," Amelie said, holding out his lead. "We're going to the park – it'll be fun!"

"Ready to go? I'm looking forward to this." Dad came out of his office, rubbing his eyes. "I've been at the computer for too long." Dad was about to go away for a conference, so he was working all hours trying to get everything done before he went. "Josh, are you sure you're not coming?"

"Homework," Josh growled from upstairs.

Dad got Monty's lead and clipped it on, and Monty followed Amelie and Maisy out of the front door. He could tell from the way they turned that they were going down the alley to the back entrance of the park and his walk got bouncier. Were they going to the field? Maybe Amelie would run with him.

But then Dad led the way on to the path round the lake instead. Monty tugged at his lead, trying to pull towards the field, but Dad just said, "Heel, Monty," and kept going. Monty followed, looking back regretfully at the long grass in the field. It was a warm day and the grass looked so cool and inviting.

Lots of people came over to make a fuss of Maisy – the park was full of dog-walkers since it was a Sunday. They were mostly people who'd seen Amelie with Monty before and they wanted to hear about the new dog. Amelie and Dad kept stopping and starting, and Monty was bored. He felt all fidgety, as though his paws were itching. He wanted to chase something.

Dad was holding him on a loose lead while they chatted to a lady with a spaniel when a pigeon walked past, right in front of his nose. Monty felt so full of energy he couldn't resist. He leaped after it, barking loudly and almost pulling the lead out of Dad's hand. The pigeon fluttered away with an indignant batting of wings. Dad stumbled, caught off balance, and put his foot down heavily right next to Maisy's back paw. Maisy yapped sharply and cowered backwards in fright.

"Monty, no!" Dad snapped, pulling him back, and Monty hunched his shoulders apologetically. Wasn't he supposed to do that? He was just so sick of standing still.

The lady with the spaniel smiled sympathetically at Monty. "He looks like he wants to get going. Good luck with them both."

"I suppose we'd better get home." Dad sighed. "Haven't you got that project to get started on, Amelie?"

"Do we have to, Dad? We were going to go for a proper long walk."

"I know, but look at Maisy. Monty really scared her."

Amelie nodded sadly. Maisy was hiding behind Dad's legs, shivering. It wasn't fair to make her walk any more if she didn't want to. "OK. Come on, Monty."

Monty stared up at Amelie in surprise. They were going home? Already? Was it because he'd chased that bird? Reluctantly, he plodded after Dad – that had hardly felt like a walk at all.

"Maisy's definitely starting to settle in," Amelie told Ella when she saw her at school on Monday. "We got Grandad to talk to her on the phone a few times over the weekend and she looks a lot happier now. She even came out for a walk with us yesterday."

"That's amazing." Ella beamed at her.

"We didn't go out for very long, though." Amelie sighed. "Monty tried to chase a pigeon and Dad tripped over and nearly trod on Maisy."

"So does Monty get on with Maisy OK?" Ella asked. "He wasn't being naughty because he's jealous of you fussing over her?"

"Of course not! Anyway, I don't

fuss over Maisy more than I do over him." *Well, maybe a little more,* a small voice inside her said. *But I have to – she's been so upset...* Amelie shook her head firmly. "Monty's fine. How's your project going? Did your mum help you with the sewing?"

She was glad when Ella rolled her eyes and started telling her about the dress disaster she was having. That little voice was still niggling away inside Amelie, telling her that maybe she had been neglecting Monty a bit...

Everyone in the class was excited about their projects – Miss Garrett said she was going to send a note home inviting parents in to see them all on Friday after school. Amelie was determined that her mosaic was going to be perfect. She had printed out a picture of a real Roman mosaic from the Internet – an under the sea scene with all sorts of fish. Amelie had decided to make just one big fish, otherwise it would take too long. Dad had gone to the craft shop and got her a big sheet of card and lots of colours of foam. It had taken ages to cut out all the little squares but now she just had to finish sticking them on top of the colour printout.

When she got home from school she laid out her box with all the coloured squares on the kitchen table and started to stick them down along the delicate arched fin on the fish's back – it was almost the last bit. She was so focused on the task that she didn't notice Monty getting up out of his basket.

The puppy had been sleeping off his dinner but he woke up feeling bright and bouncy, and spotted Amelie sitting at the kitchen table at once. He wanted her to fuss over him – or, even better, take him for a walk. He'd had a quick run with Dad that morning but he'd been in the house most of the day and Amelie hadn't taken him out when she got back from school.

Monty laid his muzzle in Amelie's lap, gazing up at her with round, hopeful eyes. He expected her to reach down and stroke his ears, like she usually did.

Instead Amelie squealed and jumped – she'd been concentrating so hard, she hadn't heard Monty coming. She caught the box of foam squares with her elbow and it went flying, pieces of foam scattering everywhere.

Monty skittered backwards. He didn't like the tiny pieces, and he snapped and clawed at them as they fell on his nose and ears.

"Oh no, Monty. Stop it!" Amelie grabbed his collar but Monty pulled away and accidentally barged into the table. Amelie's glass of water tipped over, spilling right across her picture.

"My mosaic!" Amelie wailed, letting go of Monty and trying to snatch the mosaic out of the way. But it was too late – the water had gone all over it.

"Look what you've done! Monty, you bad dog!" Amelie yelled.

Monty wriggled backwards across the kitchen, crouching low and watching Amelie out of the corner of his eye. He didn't understand what he had done but he could tell that she was angry.

There was a thumping of footsteps on the stairs and Dad hurried in. "What's the matter?"

"Look!" Amelie sniffed, wiping her hand across her eyes.

"Oh dear…" Dad picked up the mosaic, trying to brush off the worst of the water. "How did that happen?"

"Monty bumped the table," Amelie said crossly. "It's ruined. The card's going all wrinkly."

"I reckon we can rescue it." Dad looked at the mosaic thoughtfully. "I'll get your mum to pick up some more card on her way home. We can cut out the bits you've already stuck down and put them on that." He swept the stray pieces of foam into his hand. "I'll help but first I've got to finish packing for this trip tomorrow. Why don't you help me squash everything into my bag and we'll work on it later, OK?"

Amelie nodded and followed him upstairs, leaving Monty in the kitchen, gazing sadly after them. He didn't remember Amelie ever shouting at him like that before. He ducked his head as Maisy got out of her basket and came to sniff at a couple of craft-foam pieces that Dad had missed. Then she pattered over to him, her tail gently wagging. Monty licked at his muzzle nervously but Maisy didn't snap at him this time. Instead she gave his nose a friendly lick. Monty leaned down, nudging at her gratefully with his muzzle. Finally, somebody who wasn't cross with him!

Maisy trotted back to her basket and lay down but she kept glancing over at Monty. He stared back at her uncertainly. He wanted to lie down in his basket, where he felt safe, but he wanted to stay close to Maisy, too. It was the friendliest she'd ever been and she was making him feel better.

Monty crouched down at the side of his basket and pushed it with his nose across the kitchen tiles until it was next to Maisy's. Then he scrambled in and buried his head down the side of the cushion. He could hear her breathing peacefully next to him as he fell asleep.

# Chapter Five

"Morning, Amelie! Time to wake up."

Amelie peered up at her mum. "Has Dad gone?" she asked, through a yawn.

"Yes, he had to get up at four to get to the airport." Mum sighed. "I'm just going to make your packed lunches, OK?" She hurried out of the room and Amelie heard her trotting down the stairs. Usually Dad did all the school things, like their packed lunches and making sure Amelie remembered her football kit on the right days.

Amelie climbed out of bed, and then jumped as she heard a cry and a loud yelp from downstairs. "What is it?" she called anxiously, running out to lean over the banisters.

"It's that silly puppy! He's moved his basket across the kitchen and I tripped over it. Don't worry. Monty's fine – he's just surprised."

Amelie dashed downstairs to check on the puppy. Monty had sounded really panicked. He was sitting in his basket, watching Mum nervously.

"He was a bit scared by me yelling," Mum admitted. "But I didn't expect his basket to be there! I was rushing about trying to find the juice cartons for your lunch and I tripped. Oh dear… He doesn't look happy."

"Poor Monty." Amelie went over and crouched next to his basket, stroking the puppy's head. Monty licked her arm lovingly and Amelie smiled. But then she looked up and saw her mosaic, still drying on the counter. In the end Dad had said it would be best to wait before cutting it up and trying to rescue it.

Amelie sighed. It hadn't really been Monty's fault but her mosaic was never going to be as good second time round. She couldn't help feeling cross with him. She stood up sharply, pulling her hand away from him. Monty stared after her in surprise.

"I'll help you stick it back together," Josh said, coming into the kitchen and seeing her scowling at the ruined mosaic.

"Thanks." Amelie gave him a quick hug. "Mum, did you feed Monty and Maisy?"

Monty stood up in his basket, his tail wagging hopefully. He'd heard his name.

Mum shook her head. "Not yet. Sorry, dogs."

"It's OK, I'll do it." Amelie picked up both the bowls and put them on the counter, ready to pour out the dry food. Now that Monty and Maisy were more used to each other, they didn't have to eat at opposite ends of the kitchen.

Monty scampered over, eager for his breakfast. Maisy heard the dry biscuits rattling into her bowl and erupted out of her basket, ears flapping. Amelie giggled – Maisy was so funny. She was just about to put the bowls down when Monty reached over her arm and tried to gobble a mouthful. He was so hungry he stuck his nose in the wrong bowl and Amelie pulled it away.

"No—" she started to say but Maisy got there first. She snapped angrily at Monty and he darted back in fright, his ears flattening and his tail tucking between his legs.

"Maisy!" Mum cried. She took the food bowls out of Amelie's hands and put them down on the floor. "Are you all right, Amelie?"

"Yes… She wasn't anywhere near me
– she was cross with Monty because he
was trying to nick her food. She didn't
actually bite me. Or Monty." Amelie's
voice shook a little. Monty had chewed
at her fingers sometimes when he was
little but he'd never come close to
biting. She could see why Maisy had
been upset but it was still scary.

"Well, at least Monty's not hurt," Mum said. "And Maisy's forgotten about it already, look. She's eating her breakfast."

Amelie nodded. Maisy was wolfing down her food – so different to that first day when they'd brought her back from Grandad's. "I suppose she's never had to share…"

Monty had retreated to his basket again. He was hungry but he didn't want to eat next to Maisy, not after she'd snapped at him like that. Everything seemed to be going wrong. Amelie was angry with him, Mum had shouted and now Maisy had gone back to being unfriendly. He watched Amelie and Josh eating breakfast, hoping that someone would come and make a fuss of him but they were rushing to get off to school.

Quietly, he crept out of his basket and over to the kitchen door. He didn't feel like being inside any more, where everyone was cross. He slipped through the dog flap and padded down to the end of the garden to look out through the wire fence.

The field was empty, apart from a flock of starlings. Monty stood there, wagging his tail uncertainly as they hopped across the long grass. But he didn't feel like barking at them and they didn't pay any attention to the small black dog on the other side of the fence.

Monty lay curled up next to the fence, watching the comings and goings on the field. It was much busier now, with dogs going for walks. There were a few young children running about as well. Monty watched the other dogs enviously as they raced around. If only he could go for a good run like that. That little boy might even let him chase his ball.

Monty pressed his nose closer to the fence and whined, wishing the little boy would kick his ball closer. He scrabbled at the wire with one paw and then jumped back as the fence moved. It was loose at the bottom. There'd been no rain for a while and the dry, dusty earth had worn away. There was *almost* a hole.

Monty sniffed at it curiously and then scratched at the earth, sending dust flying. He whisked back, sneezing and shaking his head. The hole was bigger, definitely. This time he put his nose down and tried to squeeze it under the fence. It was tight but the wire was curling up at the bottom, and if he wriggled and pushed and scrabbled some more with his paws…

Suddenly, to his surprise, Monty shot out on the other side. He was in the field!

There was a scurry of paws behind him and a sharp warning bark. Monty looked back at the fence and saw that Maisy was there. She didn't sound angry – more confused. Maybe even a little bit frightened.

He wagged his tail at her, trying to show that everything was all right. Now that he was out in the field, with the sun warming his fur and all the delicious smells to explore, he didn't mind that she'd snapped at him.

With a friendly bark, Monty crouched down, stretching out his front paws, inviting Maisy to come and play. Perhaps she could wriggle under the fence, too? Then they could chase each other through the long grass. But Maisy only stood there and barked again. Monty looked back and forth a few times, between Maisy and that exciting stretch of grass. Then he turned his back on her and darted off into the field.

# Chapter Six

Monty pottered about, catching the scents of other dogs. Then a flash of movement caught his eye – the little boy with the ball. He was kicking it about, giggling and stumbling over the long grass.

Monty trotted up to him, and crouched down hopefully, asking the little boy to play. But the boy didn't

understand. He just stared at the
puppy, his eyes wide. Monty barked
encouragingly, hoping that the boy
would throw the ball but he didn't. He
backed away a couple of steps, looking
nervous. In the distance, the boy's
mother heard the barking. She put his
baby sister down in the pushchair and
began to run towards them.

Monty barked again but the boy still
didn't throw the ball to him. Instead
he turned and tried to run away but
in his fright he tripped up and fell
sprawling in the grass. He let out a
wail and Monty eyed him worriedly.
That wasn't a good noise. Cautiously
he padded closer and by the time the
boy's mother came running up, Monty
was standing over him.

"Leave him alone! Go away!"

Monty stepped back, tucking his tail between his legs. Why was she shouting? He'd only wanted to play. He licked his muzzle anxiously and then flinched as the mum swiped at him with the baby's teddy.

She didn't actually hit Monty but he yelped in surprise. What was going on? Now somebody else was shouting at him. He backed away, whimpering, but the frightened mum kept shouting, "Leave him! Bad dog!" and the little boy was still crying and then the baby joined in, too…

Monty turned and ran. He hadn't meant to hurt anyone and he didn't understand what he'd done wrong. All he knew was that he had to get away.

"Can we take the dogs out when we get back?" Amelie asked Josh on her way home from school. Because Dad was away and Mum was still at work, her brother had picked her up.

Josh nodded. "Yeah. Good idea. I bet Monty'd love a proper run."

Amelie was expecting Monty to come rushing up when they opened the front door – and maybe Maisy, too. But there was no patter of paws. The house was silent.

"Where are they?" she asked. Monty always came to see her as soon as she got back from school. Why wasn't he waiting for her by the door?

Amelie sighed, feeling guilty.

Maybe what Ella had hinted at was true – Monty was upset that they had a new dog. She hadn't been paying him as much attention as she usually did because she'd been worrying about Maisy. *I need to show Monty I still love him...* she thought to herself.

She hurried through the kitchen to the back door, her fingers slipping and fumbling as she tried to turn the key. As she stepped outside, she expected Monty to come running up to her – but the garden seemed to be completely empty. She ran down the path, calling, "Monty! Where are you? Maisy? Come on! Here!" She could hear Josh hurrying after her and calling, too.

Then at last Amelie saw a flash of

colour down at the end of the garden – Maisy's reddish-brown fur. The little dog came trotting up to them, wagging her tail.

Amelie patted Maisy's head but she only had half an eye on the dachshund. She still couldn't see Monty anywhere. He wasn't the sort of dog you didn't notice. She couldn't just have missed him. He wasn't there…

"Josh, I've found Maisy – look! But where's Monty?"

"He has to be here somewhere," Josh said, staring around the garden. "Maybe he's asleep under a bush…"

"But he always wakes up and comes to see us when we get home!" Amelie pointed out, her voice squeaky with panic.

"Don't stress, Amelie. I'll go and
check inside. Maybe he got shut in one
of the bedrooms or something." Josh
ran back up the garden, and Amelie
began to search up and down the lawn.

"Perhaps he went into one of the
gardens next door," Amelie suggested,
as Josh came back out, shaking his
head. "What if there's a gap in the
fence?" She stepped into the flower bed,
peering between the plants. "I can't see

any holes," she told Josh doubtfully.

"None on this side, either," he agreed. "I think we'd better call Mum – maybe she left the front door open for a minute when she went to work?"

"She won't be able to answer, though," Amelie pointed out. "She can't have her phone on her when she's out in the shop, can she?"

"No, you're right. I'll just have to leave a message. Then I'll go up and down the street, and ask if anyone's seen him."

"Josh, what if Monty's been wandering the streets for hours?" Amelie whispered. "We don't know when he got out, do we? If Mum let him out by accident, he could be miles away by now."

"You stay here and check the fence again, just in case. I'll go and ask the neighbours." Josh sped back into the house and Amelie squeezed behind the plants to look at the fence properly. She got herself tangled in a rose bush and scratched her arm but she was too worried to notice it hurting.

"Where is he, Maisy?" Amelie said, as the dachshund came to stand next to her, peering at the fence, too. "Did you see him?" Then she blinked and looked down at Maisy, thinking hard. "Maybe you did see where he went? Maisy, where's Monty?"

Maisy gazed up at her with dark, serious eyes.

Amelie sighed. "I'm being stupid, aren't I? You're not a police dog or anything… You were probably asleep in your basket, anyway."

But then the little dachshund turned round and marched out of the flower bed, as though she actually was going to find him. Amelie gazed after her for a moment – and then she scrambled out between the bushes and raced down the garden.

Maisy was in the corner right at the end, between the sweet peas Mum was growing up the fence. Her nose was practically touching the wire.

Amelie looked at Maisy doubtfully. Perhaps she'd just got bored and wandered off – but it really had looked like she understood when Amelie said Monty's name. "He's not here, Maisy," she said.

Maisy
glanced up
at her and
then scrabbled at the fence with her
neat little paws, so that the dusty earth
went flying.

Amelie crouched down, pulling at
the fence and then caught her breath in
excitement. The wire mesh was loose!
It was coming away from the post at
the bottom and there was definitely
a bit of a hole there, too. A hole that
might have been dug out...

"Is that where he went?" Amelie
asked Maisy. She was so desperate to
know what had happened, she almost
felt like the little dog might answer her.

But Maisy only sniffed at the hole
again and then stared out at the field.

# Chapter Seven

Monty shot through the gate into the main park, panting hard. His claws pattered on the tarmac path that led around the lake and he began to feel calmer. He knew this place. This was where he walked with Amelie. He liked to go sniffing along the little iron fence around the water. Amelie didn't mind – she'd stand for ages and let him catch all the smells. Monty stood resting his chin on the fence, looking across the lake. He wanted Amelie.

Monty huffed out a deep sigh and then blinked as he heard a duck quack. His tail twitched just a little from side to side and he pushed his muzzle through the fence for a closer look. There was a whole line of them coming his way, marching flatfooted around the bank.

Monty felt his tail twitch with excitement. He could scramble over the fence – or maybe even through the bars. Something deep down inside him wanted to jump the fence and run barking at the ducks so that they fluttered and flapped and quacked. But he knew he mustn't. Dad had shouted at him when he'd tried to catch that pigeon the day before.

He turned away from the fence, his head drooping. They were all cross with him. Everyone was. Even that woman had shouted at him – and he'd only been trying to play with the little boy with the ball. He trailed along the path, not sure where he was going. If he went back across the field to the garden fence, she might still be there. He didn't want to go past her again. And besides, everyone at home was angry with him, too. Maybe he shouldn't be going back there at all? But he wanted to see Amelie and Josh so much. He was hungry, too, he realized. His stomach was growling – it felt like a long time since he'd eaten. Perhaps he *should* go home...

Monty stopped and sniffed. He could smell food! He followed his nose until he came to a scattering of stale bread, piled up at the edge of the path. He started to gobble it down eagerly, even though it was old and dry.

Then, suddenly, a huge creature was there, too, snapping and hissing and flapping its wings. Monty jumped back

with a growl of fright. It was a goose.
He'd seen geese round the lake before.
Amelie always pulled him away when
they came stomping past.

Monty hated to be chased away from
the food. He had found it first, after
all! But the goose was enormous. And
now there was another one coming
and another.

They hissed and darted their beaks at him until he backed away further. He crouched under a bench, watching as they ate up all of the bread. They weren't going to leave any of it for him and his stomach was still so empty. Monty sagged down, resting his chin on his paws and gazed at them sadly.

"Josh, look! There *is* a hole! Maisy showed me."

Josh looked at the fence. "Monty couldn't get out through that. It's not big enough."

"But look, I think he dug underneath. See where the soil's all scratched away? And if he pushed this loose bit of fence, too…"

Josh shook his head. "I still reckon Mum must have let him out the front by accident. But no one's seen him – I've asked the neighbours on both sides. I think I ought to go and look for him along the next couple of streets. Can you stay here, Amelie? In case the phone rings? It's the home number on his collar – someone might find him and call. I just checked the answering machine and there aren't any messages yet but people will be coming home from work now. He might be in somebody's garden."

"All right." Amelie nodded, getting up to follow Josh into the house. "Come on, Maisy."

But Maisy didn't follow her. Amelie glanced up the garden at the house as Josh disappeared inside. She was about to go and leave Maisy behind but something held her back. The dachshund was still sniffing at the hole and looking out at the field. As Amelie watched, she clawed at the fence, pulling it back a little. There was definitely a space, even with only

Maisy's small paws working at it. Monty would have been able to pull a lot harder, Amelie thought.

"He did go out that way, didn't he?" she muttered to Maisy. She glanced uncertainly back up the garden. What if someone called, like Josh had said? But they could leave a message, after all... Amelie bit her lip, peering through the wire at the field. Maisy obviously thought Monty was out there somewhere. Maybe she could even help Amelie to find him? Amelie couldn't lose this chance – although she knew she wasn't allowed to go to the park on her own.

"I'll be back soon, I promise," she whispered, looking back towards the house. Even though Josh wasn't actually there, she felt as though she ought to explain.

Amelie nodded her head firmly. She *had* to go. She was sure that Monty had run off because of the way she'd treated him. She'd been making such a big fuss of Maisy that he must have felt like she didn't love him any more. And then she'd been so grumpy about her project!

"Maisy, stay!" Amelie dashed back into the house, grabbing Maisy's lead and then Monty's as well. Because she *was* going to find him. Then she ran back down the garden. The dachshund was clawing at the fence again, her tail wagging briskly from side to side. But she let Amelie clip on her lead.

Amelie pulled the loose edge of the fence back as far as she could and crouched down, watching as Maisy darted through the gap. Then she wriggled after the dog. The gap where the fence had come away from the post was easily big enough for Maisy, and even Monty, but it was tight for a nine-year-old girl. The loose edges of the wire caught in Amelie's hair and she panicked for a moment, sure she was stuck. Then, with a huge pull, she was free, collapsing on to the grass.

Amelie stood up, rubbing at the sore patch where her hair had pulled. "Come on, Maisy. I'm sure he's out here somewhere. Monty!"

Amelie had been racing all over the field for what seemed liked hours, with Maisy leaping in and out of the clumps of grass. She wasn't feeling nearly so certain now. There were quite a few other dogs out with their owners and Amelie had even seen a black Labrador. For a second her stomach had jumped with excitement and then she realized that the Lab was far too big.

Now they were hurrying round the lake and Amelie was peering along the banks. She was pretty sure that Monty was too big to squeeze through the bars of the little fence – but then she hadn't expected him to escape out of their garden, either.

"Sorry, Maisy," Amelie muttered. The dachshund was plodding along now, panting heavily. But she hadn't stopped, the way Amelie had seen her do with Grandad. Normally if she got tired on a walk she'd sit down solidly and sulk until someone carried her. Maisy seemed to be just as keen to keep looking as Amelie was.

"Monty doesn't like the lake as much as the field," Amelie said, crouching down for a moment to rub Maisy's silky ears. "But he likes watching the ducks. Maybe he did come this way. Oh, I just don't know! And we've been out for ages, Josh must have got back by now…"

She stood up, looking back and forth between the lake path and the opening in the hedge that led back to the field. What should they do?

"Just a quick look," she said to Maisy at last. "We can't give up yet, we just can't. Monty ran away because of me and now I've got bring him home."

# Chapter Eight

Monty lay huddled under the bench in the shady patch where a huge buddleia bush had started to grow over the seat. The geese had gone now but he hadn't come out of his hiding place. It seemed better to stay where he was, even though he was so hungry. He let out a great, heavy sigh and wriggled on the dusty tarmac until he was a bit more comfortable. He was tired after all that running and the fright from the geese. The bees buzzing in the purple flowers over his head were making him feel sleepy, too…

Monty had almost drifted off when he heard them. The busy clicking of little clawed paws and Amelie's voice calling. Calling *him*!

"Monty! Monty! Here, boy!"

They were just a bit further round the path. Monty shook his head sleepily and almost leaped out from under the bench. But then he woke up a little more and something stopped him. Amelie had been so cross before – maybe he shouldn't go to her. But he *wanted* to! He shuffled forwards uncertainly, peering out between the branches. He wanted Amelie to pat him and pull his ears that special way she did and tell him he was a good boy. But what if she didn't? Maisy was with Amelie, too – and Amelie never seemed to be cross with *her*.

Monty whined – he just didn't know what to do. But then he heard Amelie calling again and something in her voice made him scramble out from under the bench. He didn't care if she was still cross. He had to go back to her.

He was shaking the dust and bits of twig out of his fur when he saw them running towards him, Maisy trotting ahead with her tail wagging eagerly and Amelie hurrying after her. Monty looked up at Amelie, uncertain but hopeful, his tail beating slowly from side to side.

"Oh, Monty! We were so worried about you!" Amelie crouched down beside him and brushed a bit of dirt off his nose. "Please don't ever do that again."

Her voice was trembling and Monty eyed her uncertainly. She didn't sound angry with him but she didn't sound like her usual self, either. He nosed at her hand and she laughed. "We didn't know where you were," she whispered, running her hand over his head over and over again. "I was so scared. I'm sorry I was grumpy with you. It wasn't your fault about my project. I know you just wanted me to fuss over you like I'd been fussing over Maisy."

Monty sat down and leaned against her knees, loving the soothing murmur of her voice.

"I bet you're starving," Amelie said suddenly. "Monty, do you want dinner?" She giggled as he jumped up, his tail wagging like mad. "That'll be a yes, then. Oh, and we should get back and tell Josh we've found you!" She clipped on Monty's lead and hurried the two dogs back round the lake towards the gate that led out to the alleyway.

Amelie rang the front doorbell in one long peal. Then she peered through the glass, trying to see her brother coming to answer the door.

"I'm behind you!"

Amelie jumped round to find Josh running up the path, grinning at her.

"You found him! Where was he? Wow, Monty, I've been looking all over for you!" He crouched down to stroke the puppy, while Monty whined delightedly and scrabbled at his knees. Josh fussed over him for a moment and then looked up at Amelie, frowning. "Hang on! You're supposed to be in the house in case someone phones! Where have you been?"

Amelie folded her arms and glared. "I got him back, Josh! He *had* gone out through that hole in the fence – he was in the park. Maisy was right…" Then she spotted Monty's anxious eyes and softened her voice. "I know I shouldn't have gone on my own."

Josh sighed. "At least he's home. I'd better leave Mum another message. I don't know what I'm going to tell her, though."

"I really am sorry, Josh. Maisy was so sure. She pulled the fence up with her paw and I was certain she knew where Monty had gone. I didn't want to miss the chance of finding him."

Josh nodded and pulled out his keys. "I won't say anything to Mum. But don't ever do anything like that again, OK?"

Monty barked encouragingly as the keys jangled and Maisy gave an excited little yap.

"Yes, all right, you both want dinner. Come on then!" Josh unlocked the door and the two dogs rushed in, jumping around Amelie's feet while she tried to take off their leads.

"I'll get the food ready," Josh called, heading into the kitchen. "Amelie, just look at Maisy. Think back to a week ago!"

Amelie beamed as she finally managed to unclip the lead from Maisy's collar and the dachshund licked her cheek. "I know," she said, following the two dogs into the kitchen. "But I feel really bad, Josh. I was worrying so much about her I forgot about Monty. He thought no one loved him any more."

Josh put the food bowls down – side by side – and watched as the two dogs tucked in. They didn't look bothered about eating right next to each other at all. "I guess you're probably right," he admitted. "We did neglect him – even though we didn't mean to."

Monty licked out the last crumbs

from his food bowl, cleaning it so
thoroughly that it went scraping across
the floor. He looked at it for a moment,
in case some more food suddenly
appeared – and then he yawned so
widely that Amelie could see every one
of his teeth. He gave the bowl one last
sniff and padded wearily over to his
basket, climbing in and slumping down.

Maisy inspected her bowl and then
pattered across the tiles after him.
Their baskets were still next to each
other but she didn't climb into hers
at once. She stood there, looking at
Monty, who was lying with his nose
hanging out over the side of his huge
basket. Maisy came a little closer and
then hopped in with him, curling up
in front of Monty's tummy.

Amelie held her breath. Monty lifted up his head to stare at Maisy and he seemed a bit surprised but he didn't look as though he minded. He laid his head down again and lifted one long black paw, draping it lovingly over Maisy's side.

"He's hugging her!" Amelie whispered.

Josh pulled out his phone to take a picture. "I'm sending this one to Grandad."

"She's like a different dog," Grandad said, smiling at Amelie. "Having a puppy like Monty to play with has taken years off her. Look at her go!"

Amelie nodded. Maisy was galloping down the garden towards them, chasing Monty, who had a rubber bone in his mouth.

"She's hardly touching the ground," Amelie giggled. "Look at her flappy ears! I think she's going to take off."

Monty skidded up to them and dropped the bone in front of Amelie, who was sitting by Grandad's feet.

"You're so clever!" Amelie rubbed his nose. "Shall I throw it again? Are you going to let Maisy fetch it this time?" She waved the bone at him and then threw it down the garden. Monty hurled himself after it.

"Ha!" Grandad laughed. "Maisy's got a strategy. She's not coming all the way back up here, she's waiting halfway so she can get to it first. Maisy, that's cheating!"

"She's allowed to cheat a bit," Mum pointed out, handing Grandad a mug of tea.

Josh reached over to grab a glass of juice from the tray. "Yeah, look how much shorter her legs are."

"Don't you miss her, Grandad?" Amelie asked suddenly. Then she wished she hadn't – she didn't want to make Grandad sad. But she couldn't imagine giving up Monty and she'd only had him for a few months. Maisy had been Grandad's dog for years.

"Of course I do." Grandad sighed. "But I wasn't taking her on enough walks, Amelie. She's better off here. I'm really settled in my new flat and there are people around to look after me if I need it but I still get to see Maisy. It's the best of both worlds."

"It's been brilliant for Monty, too," Amelie said, smiling as Maisy whipped the bone out from under Monty's nose. "He loves having her to play with, especially when we're at school."

Mum nodded. "I think we might have to get a bigger basket. Maisy never sleeps in hers any more and Monty's growing so fast they won't both fit in his soon."

Maisy hurtled up the garden towards them and dropped the bone triumphantly next to Grandad's feet. Then she sat down between him and Amelie, panting heavily and looking delighted with herself.

Monty trotted up to them and nudged his nose against Maisy's. Then he slumped down on Amelie's other side, resting his head on her bare feet. He didn't mind about not getting to the bone first – not that much – but he wanted everyone to know that Amelie belonged to him.

Amelie giggled as the whiskery underside of his muzzle tickled her toes. "You're such a good boy, Monty," she whispered. "You know that, don't you?"

# The Story Puppy

For Hattie

# Chapter One

Jack stared down at the page in front of him. The words seemed to be getting all blurry round the edges and he blinked hard. He was not going to cry. He was not.

It wouldn't have been quite so bad if it were Mr Gardner, their teacher, that he was trying to read with. But it was Amarah's mum.

Jack had been really pleased when Amarah told him her mum was coming to help out with hearing their class read. He liked Amarah's mum – he'd known her for years, ever since Amarah's family had moved in next door.

It was different now that Amarah's mum was trying to get him to read out loud, though. Every time he saw her over the fence, he was going to remember sitting here. He'd been fighting to read this sentence for what felt like hours.

"Try and sound it out," Amarah's mum said gently.

"I can't," Jack muttered.

"I bet you can if you try."

"No, I can't!" Jack banged the book down on the table. Stupid book! He'd thought it would be good, when he picked it. He loved dogs and the book had a photo of a glossy golden retriever on the front. The dog's dark eyes looked right at him and its tongue was hanging out, as though it had just been for a run.

It shouldn't be so hard – all Jack wanted to do was read about the dog. But the words just kept swimming away.

"Maybe we should take a break?" Mrs Iqbal suggested. "You've worked really hard today, Jack."

Jack didn't say anything. He fixed his eyes on the edge of the table, hoping the bell was going to ring. Waiting for Mr Gardner to say it was someone else's turn to read. What made it worse was that he *had* worked really hard – he'd been trying and trying. But it was no good. The words just didn't make sense.

Mrs Iqbal glanced round. "Oh – there's Elsa. It's her turn to read next."

Jack was almost sure she was glad to get rid of him.

Jack slouched back down the corridor to his classroom. The rest of the class were doing maths and he was good at maths. Numbers did what they ought to, not like letters. But he was still feeling miserable, and antsy, and cross. He didn't want to sit down and work out fractions. Mr Gardner would notice if he didn't get back soon, though, and their head teacher, Mrs Bellamy, had a spooky habit of turning up whenever anyone wasn't in the right place.

Glumly, Jack opened the door to the Year Five classroom.

Mr Gardner waved at him and said, "Amarah, can you show Jack where we're up to on the worksheet, please?"

Amarah nodded importantly and as Jack slumped into the chair beside her, she started to point out the questions they'd been doing.

"All right," he muttered, grabbing a pencil.

"What's up with you?" Amarah asked, peering at him curiously.

"Nothing."

"Was it the reading?" Amarah sounded sympathetic and Jack knew she was trying to be nice, but that didn't help. It wasn't fair! Why was it so much harder for him than for anybody else? And what if Amarah's mum told her that he hadn't been able to read? Then Amarah would think he was stupid. Jack's eyes started to sting again and just in that minute he felt so angry with Amarah. And her mum.

"My reading's fine," he snapped. "Leave me alone!"

"Don't be mean!" One of Amarah's other friends, Lily, pointed her pencil at him. "Amarah's only trying to be nice."

Jack glared at her. "Just keep out of it, Lily. And stop waving that at me," he added, smacking the pencil out of her hand.

He had only meant to stop her from waggling the pencil about – he thought it would just land on the table. Instead, it sailed across the room and hit Mr Gardner's trousers.

"Now look what you've done!" said Lily. She sounded half horrified and half excited. "You're going to get in trouble."

"Oh no…" Amarah whispered, watching nervously as Mr Gardner came over to their table.

"Since you all look guilty, I'm guessing this came from one of you?" Mr Gardner said, sighing.

"Sorry, Mr Gardner," Jack muttered, staring at the table. "It was an accident."

"No, it wasn't," Lily put in and

Amarah elbowed her.

"Be more careful, Jack. I'm watching this table." Mr Gardner stood there for a moment longer, as though he wanted to say something else, but then the bell rang for lunch.

"What did you do that for?" Amarah whispered to Jack as she came to stand behind him in the line for lunch.

"Leave me alone!" Jack hissed back. And then when Amarah looked like she was going to keep on talking, he darted out of his place and went further down the line to stand with Mason and James instead.

But all through lunch he could feel Amarah watching him. She was sitting with Lily, like she usually did, but she kept glancing over at him and she looked miserable. Really miserable and confused, as if she didn't know what she'd done wrong.

Jack didn't eat very much lunch.

The puppy flinched anxiously back among the weeds as another car roared past. She didn't understand what was happening. Were her people coming back? She'd tried to run after them when their car pulled away, but it was going much too fast and she was limping. She'd landed badly when they'd pushed her out of the car door – she hadn't expected it and she'd banged hard against the tarmac.

She lifted up her paw now and licked at it, whining softly. She knew the way the car had gone but she wasn't sure she could walk much further, not with her leg like this. She'd have to wait for them to come back.

She hoped it would be soon. She was so hungry and it felt like ages since she'd had anything to eat. The people had taken her mother away the day before, so she couldn't have milk and they hadn't given her any dry food that morning either.

The puppy had howled half the night with misery and she still didn't know where her mother was. She was hungry and lonely and frightened, and she didn't know what to do.

She huddled back again as the next car approached, but this time the car slowed down as it passed her. It slowed down even more, and then stopped.

The puppy wagged her tail uncertainly. Had her people come back? Perhaps her mother was in the car! She wagged a little harder and tried to sniff the air. She knew her mother's smell, but the scent was all mixed up with the dusty road and the sharp whiff of cars...

"Hey, sweetie … are you lost?"
Someone climbed out of the car and
began to walk towards her. The puppy
looked uncertainly up and down the
road. This was a stranger, she was
almost sure. Should she try to run? But
her paw… She whimpered and the
man approaching her slowed down and
began to talk again, his voice very soft.

"It's OK. Did you run off, little
thing? You're ever so skinny… Don't
be scared…" He crouched down a

271

little way in front of her and held out his hand. "Where's home then?" he murmured. "Come on, puppy, it's OK… Come and see me…"

The gentle voice burbled on and the puppy wagged her tail again. She didn't know him, but he was slow and quiet and he sounded kind. He might even have food and she was so, so hungry.

Hopping on three paws, the puppy struggled over to the edge of the road and sniffed his outstretched fingers. When the man picked her up and snuggled her against his jacket, she just sighed and nuzzled in. He was warm and he smelled gentle, and she didn't know what else to do.

# Chapter Two

Jack was in the garden, curled up at the top of the battered old slide, when he heard the back door bang.

"Are you up there?" his sister called. "Mum says do you want a banana?"

"Hate bananas," Jack growled. He didn't actually, but at the moment he didn't feel like saying yes to anything. He'd got into trouble for accidentally on purpose kicking Mason's football too hard against a window at lunch break, and he'd kept on feeling grim and angry all afternoon.

"OK." There was a creaking sound and Mattie pulled herself the wrong way up the slide and came to sit next to him. It was a tight fit with two, but Jack was glad she hadn't gone away. Mattie didn't say anything, just closed her eyes and sat leaning back against the wooden slats.

"Are you OK?" Jack asked. She looked really tired.

"Got an essay to write." Mattie sighed. She was at college doing her A levels and it seemed like a lot of work to Jack. Mattie was always stressing about essays, and she had to fit them in round weekend shifts at the supermarket and helping out at the animal shelter down the road. "I'm putting it off, but I've got to get it started before I go to the shelter. How about you?"

Jack didn't say anything. He hadn't told Mum about his awful day, though he thought she'd probably guessed something was wrong by the way he'd marched out of school glowering at everyone. Then he sighed. Mattie was easy to talk to. She didn't look worried like Mum, or start trying to think of loads of ways to help. Mum was only being nice when she did that, but sometimes it made Jack feel worse.

"School was…" He stopped, trying to think how to put it.

"Not good?"

"Bad," he admitted, staring at his hands. "You know Amarah's mum helps out sometimes?" He waved at Amarah's garden over the fence – it was beautiful, full of roses.

"Mmm. With the reading?"

"Yeah. She was listening to me read – except I couldn't." Jack glanced sideways at Mattie. "The book was really difficult," he whispered. His voice was hoarse, as if he were about to cry. It was so hard saying it. "Difficult for me, I mean. Probably anyone else in my class could have read it."

Mattie slipped an arm round his shoulders. "I bet there are people in your class who aren't good at other things. You're really good at maths."

"Even in maths you have to read the questions," Jack muttered.

Mattie sighed. "I suppose so."

"It was horrible. I felt stupid and I didn't know what to say. Amarah's mum was really nice about it, but I bet she thinks I'm useless now. And what if she says something to Amarah?" Jack's voice shook.

"I don't think she'd do that," Mattie said comfortingly. "Look, can I read with you sometimes? Mr Gardner said it was partly just practice you needed. When he had that meeting with Mum about you getting help with your reading."

Jack leaned against her shoulder, feeling grateful. "That would be good," he agreed.

"OK. Do you feel like doing it now?" Mattie peered sideways at him, a bit doubtfully. "Or maybe when you're feeling better? We could do it before bedtime when I get back from the shelter?"

"Yeah…" Jack nodded. He could see that Mattie wanted to help, but when was she going to find the time? She was so busy with her college work and her job. And whenever she had a spare moment she went to the animal shelter to help walk the dogs or sit and stroke the cats. She'd told Jack that sometimes they needed reminding that people were nice. It seemed sad the cats had to be shown that, but Jack had visited the shelter with Mattie and he'd seen how hard the staff worked. They didn't have time to give the dogs and cats all the fuss and love they needed.

Maybe he should ask Mum to help him with reading instead, Jack thought as Mattie shot down the slide and went inside to get on with her homework. Mum always offered, but usually Jack did everything he could to get out of it – saying he was tired, or he had maths homework to do, or it was sunny so could he go outside and

play with Amarah? He hated it when
he got words wrong and Mum looked
so worried. It made the words even
harder to understand.

The puppy was hiding. This pen was
more comfortable than the one she'd
been kept in before – there was a soft
bed and a clean water bowl and more
food than she'd ever had. But it was
different and it smelled strange. It was
noisy too – there were so many other
dogs here, all barking and howling
and whining. Every time she settled
down in the cosy bed, someone
would start to bark and she'd leap
up shivering.

The puppy had nudged her bed towards the back of the pen, squashing it up against the corner. It was big enough that if she hopped over the top and curled up tight, no one could see her – or she hoped they couldn't. The hard floor wasn't that comfortable, but she felt better tucked away.

The man who'd picked her up by the side of the road had brought her here. She'd huddled up on the car seat next to him, wrapped in his coat but still shivering. The car had growled and shuddered and she'd hated it. What if he stopped and threw her out of the door, just as her people had? When the car's engine finally died away and he reached over to pick her up, she'd cowered away from him with a whine.

The man had carried her into this place, murmuring to her gently, but then he'd left her. He went away and strangers had bandaged up her leg. It had hurt. They'd fed her and stroked her and fussed over her, but she didn't understand what was happening. Were her people going to come back? Where was her mother? Why were all these other dogs here?

The puppy whimpered and wriggled her nose underneath the padded dog bed. It was dark there and warm. She wriggled in further and she could almost not hear the barking.

Amarah grabbed the sleeve of Jack's sweater and pulled him ahead. Jack's mum was walking them all to school, but she was busy talking to Amarah's little sister Anika.

"What was wrong with you yesterday?" Amarah demanded, once they'd got far enough in front. "Why were you being so horrible?"

"I wasn't!" Jack protested, but he knew she was right.

"I had art club after school or I'd have talked to you then. You can't just pretend nothing happened. You were lucky Mr Gardner didn't send you out of the class."

Jack looked down at the pavement. "I know," he muttered eventually. "Thanks for trying to stop Lily telling."

"You did hit her pencil across the room. You can't blame her."

Jack only nodded and Amarah rolled her eyes at him. "So what made you so cross? It wasn't just Lily. You were angry before she said anything."

Jack's shoulders drooped and he kicked the pavement with his toe. "It was your mum," he whispered at last. "Don't get upset!" he added quickly. "It wasn't her fault. She didn't do anything bad – she was hearing me read."

Amarah looked at him for a moment. Then she said, "I thought you liked my mum!" in a hurt voice.

"I do!" Jack said, almost in a wail. "But I couldn't read the book and she must have thought I was stupid. I was worried she would tell you."

"Oh…" Amarah looked thoughtful. "Well, she didn't. She said she'd had you for reading, but the only thing she told me about yesterday was that one of the girls in Year Two nearly threw up on her shoes."

"What?" Jack gasped.

"Uh-huh. Mum got her feet out of the way just in time. But when I asked who it was, she said it wouldn't be fair to tell me. She wouldn't say mean things about you either, even if she thought them. And I bet she didn't." Amarah frowned, wrinkling her nose. "Actually, I've just remembered, she said she thought you'd had your hair cut and it looked nice."

"Oh…" Jack blinked. He'd been almost positive that Amarah's mum would tell her how terrible his reading was. He'd seen them talking about it so clearly in his head. It took him a little while to realize he'd imagined the whole story.

Amarah nodded. Then she added, "What was wrong with the reading?"

Jack shrugged, but then he muttered, "Don't know. I just can't do it."

"Was Mum any help?"

"Ummm. Not really. Sorry." Jack glanced up at her anxiously. He really didn't want to upset Amarah again, but she just looked thoughtful.

"So ... what are you going to do?"

"Practise with Mum. Mattie said she'd help too, but I don't think she'll have time with all her school stuff and going to the shelter. And work. She's never in. I was nearly asleep by the time she got back last night."

Jack sighed. "What else can I do?"

"I don't know." Amarah shook her head. "I'll think about it, though. There must be something."

"Maybe." But Jack looked doubtful.

# Chapter Three

Mattie slumped down on the sofa next to Jack. "Want to do some reading now?" she asked, smothering a yawn. "I've got time."

Jack felt himself tensing up, but he nodded. "I'll get the book." He was still trying to work his way through the one with the golden retriever on the cover, but he wasn't enjoying it much. It was

too hard to get into the story and he
kept forgetting what had happened.
He had read with Mattie and Mum a
couple of times over the weekend, and
he thought it might be helping, but it
was all so difficult.

He and Mattie struggled through
a page to the end of the chapter and
looked at each other hopefully. "We
could stop there?" Jack suggested and
Mattie nodded.

"Mum's making dinner. It'll be ready in a minute."

"Did you go to the shelter after college today?" Jack asked.

"Uh-huh."

"What's the matter?" Now that he looked at her properly, Mattie seemed really upset – Jack hadn't even noticed. His big sister tried not to tell him about the sad bits of working at the shelter, but he knew she came home worrying about the cats and dogs a lot. Mattie rested her chin on her hands and heaved a sigh. "It's one of the new dogs," she explained. Then she looked round at him. "You're sure you want me to tell you?"

"Yes…" Jack said, a little doubtfully.

"She's a puppy. Really little and

so sweet. She's white and a bit fluffy – she's probably got some Maltese in her, Lucy thinks." Lucy was the manager at the shelter. "I named her." Mattie smiled, but then her smile faded. "She's called Daisy."

"Why are you sad, if she's so sweet?" Jack asked, hugging himself tightly. He almost wished he hadn't let Mattie start telling him.

"Lucy says she's not sure we'll ever be able to rehome her."

"Why? What's the matter with her?" Jack frowned. Mattie was always telling him how the shelter staff were desperate to find good homes for all the animals. She really wanted them to adopt a dog, but Mum wasn't sure, with everyone in the family so busy with work and school. She didn't think they'd be able to look after a dog very well. Jack thought they'd be fine – every time he went to the shelter with Mattie he fell in love with a different dog, but they hadn't managed to persuade Mum yet.

"She's so nervous and miserable," Mattie explained. "She won't go to anyone and she hides whenever we bring her food or we come to clean out her pen. She doesn't trust people and she seems to hate being touched. I suppose someone was horrible to her. We get nervous dogs all the time – and dogs that are upset because their owners have died – and they hate being in the shelter. But usually they start to get a bit friendlier after a while. That's not happening with Daisy. She's been at the shelter a week and she still won't let any of us come near her. She's such a little dog – only a baby! It's not fair!"

"Oh…" Jack leaned against Mattie's shoulder. "That's really sad."

"I wish I could help her," Mattie murmured. "But I just don't know how."

Mattie was picking Jack up from school the next day – Amarah had art club and Mum was working – so she took him with her to the shelter. Jack helped out, filling up food bowls in the kitchen, and then he went for a wander around. He knew all the staff and most of the volunteers by now and no one minded him being there as long as he didn't upset any of the animals.

He tried to make a fuss of a couple of cats, but they were dozing and only peered sleepily at him when he crouched down outside their pens. There was a whole litter of black and white kittens, though, who were more interesting. Jack watched them for a while, laughing as they stalked each other's tails across the pen and then collapsed and fell asleep in a furry bundle on the floor.

After that, he went to visit the dogs. He'd seen most of them before. There were a couple of elderly dogs that nobody seemed to want to adopt – they'd been at the shelter for months. Jack's favourite was a wheezy, fawn-coloured pug. No one had been

feeling very imaginative the day he
was brought in, so he was just called
Pug. He met Jack with excited squeaky
barks and Jack sat down on the floor
by his pen and stroked him through
the wire.

Pug stood
there with
his eyes
closed and
his curled
tail whirring
while Jack
scratched
his ears and
under his
chin.

"Five more minutes, OK?" Mattie
said, hurrying past. "Just got to help

Lucy finish feeding everybody."

"OK," said Jack, then he had a thought. "Hey, Mattie!"

She turned round, walking backwards with her arms full of food bowls. "What?"

"Which pen is the new puppy in?"

Mattie stopped. "Daisy?"

Jack nodded. "I just wanted to see her…" he murmured. He hadn't been able to stop thinking about the little white puppy, since Mattie had told him how unhappy she was.

"She's not any better, Jack. Lucy told me. You'll just be upset seeing her."

"I don't care," Jack said stubbornly. "If you didn't want me knowing about her, why did you tell me?"

Mattie sighed. "I shouldn't have done.

OK… She's in the pen at the end. It's the quietest one. She doesn't seem to like the other dogs barking. I'm about to go and put her food bowl in, actually. You can come with me. Just … just don't scare her, all right?"

"Of course I won't!" Jack said indignantly. But then he nodded. "I promise I won't, Mattie. I only want to see her."

"You'll be lucky if you do," Mattie said over her shoulder as she went on down the passage. "When I went past earlier, she was hiding underneath her bed."

Jack made one last fuss of Pug and then got up to follow her. All the dogs knew it was time for their dinner and they were watching excitedly as Mattie came along with the bowls. She slipped into the pens, talking lovingly to each of the dogs as she gave them their food. Mostly they tried to eat it before she had even put the bowl down. But when they got to the pen at the end, as far as Jack could see, it was empty. Then he remembered what Mattie had said about the puppy being under her bed. It did look a bit lumpy in the middle. Was there really a puppy there, too scared to come out?

Mattie quietly opened the pen and put down the bowl. Then she came out again, looking worried. "We'll wait here for a bit," she said to Jack, beckoning him to come a little further down the passage, where they could just about see Daisy's pen. "I want to make sure she's OK. And check she's actually eating her dinner."

Jack nodded and they both stood there, craning their necks sideways. After a minute or two, the dog bed shifted a little and a whiskery white face appeared. Daisy looked around cautiously for a moment or two and then pattered across the pen to her bowl. But she kept darting anxious glances at the passage, as if she thought something scary was about to happen.

"She's so small!" Jack breathed in Mattie's ear.

"I know. She's probably about eight weeks. That's only just old enough to leave her mum. Isn't she sweet? She'd be adopted straightaway if she wasn't so timid."

Jack's stomach seemed to turn over inside him. Mattie had said that the puppy had been dumped by the side of the road. He couldn't imagine who would do that to such a tiny dog. Looking at her now, shivering as she tried to eat, he decided he'd do anything, anything to make her better.

Daisy was almost sure that someone was watching her eat. She could smell people – or thought she could. The smells here were all so strange and strong. The sharp scent of the spray the staff used to clean the pens seemed to sting her nose.

Whoever it was didn't come any

closer, though, so she kept bolting down the food. The faster she ate, the faster she could hide herself away again. She didn't want anyone to notice her. It was safe there, tucked under her bed in the warm and the dark. It reminded her of being snuggled up with her mother. And even though the hard floor of the pen made her bruised paw hurt, it was definitely better being under the bed than in it.

She licked quickly round the bowl and darted away, burrowing back underneath the squashy bed. Then she lay there, listening, tense all over, until she heard the footsteps going away.

# Chapter Four

Jack had only seen Daisy for a couple of minutes, but he couldn't stop thinking about her. She was tiny, and white all over, with soft ears and a stubby, scruffy little tail. Mattie said that breakfast and dinner were the only times they really saw her – two minutes of desperate gobbling, before she scurried back to hide under her bed.

"Lucy and Adrian have both spent as much time with her as they can," she'd explained to Jack. Adrian was the other full-time member of staff at the shelter. "Lucy goes in and just sits in the pen for ages. She's hoping that Daisy will get used to her being there and come out. Though she hasn't so far. But they're so busy – the shelter's full again. Any time they spend coaxing Daisy to be friendly is time they have to take away from the other dogs and cats."

It didn't seem fair to Jack that Daisy needed help and everyone was too busy to give it to her. He wished *he* could help. But he wasn't old enough to be an official volunteer at the shelter. He didn't know anything about helping a dog like Daisy either. He'd probably get it all wrong. But he definitely wanted to see her again – even if all he saw was a little hump under her bed.

So the next day, instead of going home with Amarah and her mum and Anika, he persuaded Mattie to come and pick him up. He told Amarah why on the way to school that morning – he didn't want her to think he was abandoning her. Once he had told her about Daisy, though, she was all for it.

"Can you take a picture of her?" she asked. "Mattie could take one on her phone, couldn't she?"

"Maybe while she's eating," Jack said. "Otherwise it'll be a photo of a dog bed."

"That's so sad. I wish I could come with you. I want to go to the shelter anyway. Maybe we could persuade my mum and dad to get a cat."

"I could ask Mattie to take you with us one day?" Jack suggested.

Amarah nodded. Then she looked at Jack, chewing her lip as though she wasn't sure what to say. "Did you finish that book?"

"Almost…" Jack muttered. Mr Gardner had checked on their reading diaries the day before, and he'd done his *I'm very disappointed* face when he realized Jack was still in the middle of the book about the golden retriever.

"Mr Gardner said to do it last night!"

"Yeah, but I was at the shelter with Mattie." Jack shrugged. "I bet he didn't think I would anyway. He knows I'm useless at reading."

Amarah eyed him doubtfully. "He sounded like he meant it to me. I hope you don't get told off again."

Jack looked worried for a moment and then he grinned at Amarah. "I won't. We've got that history day, remember? There are people coming in to do a workshop. I'll finish the reading tonight. No problem."

"You'd better," Amarah said seriously. "I like our table the way it is – if you keep getting in trouble we'll all be moved round again and I'll end up sitting next to Lola or somebody else mean."

"All right, I will, I promise!" Jack sighed. "You're worse than Mr Gardner."

"Do you want to help with getting the food ready again?" Mattie suggested.

"Definitely." Jack nodded. The more he did to help out, the more time Mattie and the others would have to spend with the animals. It was called socializing. Jack hadn't really got it when Mattie had explained it to him before, but now he saw how much love and attention Daisy needed.

He measured out the food for Mattie while she ferried the bowls to the pens. They'd finished getting all the dogs' dinners ready when Mattie suddenly stopped, frowning at him. "Hang on. I've just remembered. Haven't you got homework to do? Amarah said I had to make sure you finished your book."

"I can do it later!" Jack protested.

"Uh-uh. We'll get home, you'll have dinner, you'll be really tired – you won't have time to finish it. Just go and sit in the visitors' room now."

Jack glared at her, but then he gave a massive huffy sigh and went to get his backpack. Mattie was right, though. And so was Amarah – he didn't want Mr Gardner moving them around in class either.

He was searching through his backpack for the reading book when it struck him – he had to do the reading, but it didn't matter *where* he did it. Mattie had said that Lucy went and sat in Daisy's pen to try and get her used to people. He couldn't do that – Lucy would definitely say no, in case Daisy

311

got really scared and nipped him –
but he could sit just outside her pen,
couldn't he? That would be almost as
good. He could sit still and not scare her,
and even though he had to sound out a
lot of the words he could do it quietly.

Jack hurried down the passage to the
pen at the end and sat down, leaning
against the wall. The floor was a bit hard,
but it wasn't too bad. Besides, Daisy was
lying on that hard floor all day.

"Hey, Daisy," he whispered. He
could just about see the end of her
tail sticking out from under the dog
bed. "Are you OK? I've got to finish
this reading homework, so I thought
I'd do it with you." He looked at the
bump under the bed for a moment
– almost as though he thought she

might answer him. Then he shook his head and opened up the book, flicking through the pages to the right place. He was a *long* way from the end.

"OK. So. Page forty-six. 'Benny … pushed the gate shut with his nose…'" Jack read on, slowly sounding out the hardest words.

He wasn't sure if Mr Gardner would think reading to a dog counted as reading with an adult – especially since Daisy was only a puppy and she wasn't actually listening – but Jack liked it more than reading to Mum or Mattie. He knew Daisy was there, so it still felt like he was reading to someone, but she didn't mind if he got the words wrong or took ages to work them out.

Mattie fidgeted when he read to her. He was pretty sure she didn't know she was doing it, but she always fiddled with the hem of her sweater or jiggled her feet around like she was bored. Mum sat still, but she tried to help too much. She was always telling him not to worry, when he wasn't – *she* was the one who was worrying.

He got to the end of the page and
stopped for a rest, stretching out
his shoulders. He'd been hunching
forward, peering at the book. Then he
froze. There had been a flash of white
inside the pen. He was sure of it.

Had Daisy moved?

There was no sign of her now –
except for that little wisp of white tail
sticking out.

Slowly, Jack started to read again.
He kept his face down towards the
book, but every so often he rolled
his eyes sideways to look into the
pen. He was about halfway down
the next page – and how had that
happened? It felt like the fastest
he'd ever managed to read anything
– when a black nose appeared from

under the dog bed and the stub of tail disappeared. Daisy was wriggling forward. She was listening!

Jack went on. He wasn't sure he'd be able to tell Mr Gardner what happened on any of those pages, he was too busy keeping an eye on Daisy, but he *was* reading. And he liked that he was reading about a dog to a dog.

After a few more sentences, the rest of Daisy's muzzle edged out from under the bed and he could just see her dark eyes glinting at him from under the fabric.

"Oh…" he murmured a couple of minutes later. "Only one more chapter to go. Do you like this story?" He peered at Daisy again and went on talking quietly. There was more of her sticking out now. He could see her collar, and her front paws were showing too, one on each side of her nose. Jack flicked the pages over. The last chapter was short, only a couple of pages. He could do that. Definitely.

By the time he'd got to the very end of the book, Daisy was still lying on the floor, but only half of her was under her bed. She lay watching Jack with her nose on her crossed front paws and she really seemed to be listening. As if she was actually enjoying listening to him read. Jack couldn't remember the last time that had happened.

# Chapter Five

Daisy could hear someone talking outside her pen. It was a quiet voice, speaking rather slowly. Some of the people here had tried to talk to her before – they'd sat in her pen and tried to coax her to come out and see them. She never did. She came out for food and ate it as fast as she could, but that was all. Once the lights were off and the staff had left, she crept out and snuggled on top of her bed. But at the slightest noise – another dog barking or even just shifting in its sleep – she would be straight back underneath.

Whoever was talking now hadn't tried to come in to her space. She liked that. They stopped every now and then, the sounds stumbling out. It made the noise seem gentle and she liked that too. It was hard to hear, though, underneath her bed.

Very slowly, she edged forward so that her nose stuck out. The boy's reading was clearer now, but then he stopped talking and she whisked back to the safe darkness under the bed. Slowly, quietly, he started again and Daisy wriggled out, centimetre by centimetre.

Apart from the quiet, halting voice, the dog section of the shelter was almost silent. No one was barking. Daisy let her ears flop down and she rested her muzzle gently on her paws. The fear that had been building up inside her for days eased, just a little, and her eyes half closed as Jack went on.

Jack didn't tell Mattie what had happened – he still wasn't sure he believed it anyway. It could just have been a coincidence that Daisy happened to decide to come out of her hiding place just then. But he really, really hoped not. If it was actually him helping, he had to go there again. Mattie wasn't going to be at the shelter for the next couple of days – she had shifts at the supermarket – but she always fitted in helping at the weekend. And he was going to go with her.

"Are you sure?" Mattie eyed him sleepily at breakfast on Saturday morning. "You know I'm going now

– before I have to go to work? As in, you'd better be dressed in three minutes if you really want to come?"

Jack didn't need to think about it. He dashed upstairs and threw on some clothes. He was back in the kitchen before Mattie had got halfway through her cereal.

"Is that OK, Mattie?" Mum asked, stirring her tea. "Jack won't be in your way?"

"I'm helpful!" Jack pointed out, feeling annoyed. "I put the food out for the dogs, and on Wednesday..." He trailed off. He'd forgotten he wasn't going to tell anyone about Daisy.

"On Wednesday what?" Mum asked.

"On Wednesday I did my homework at the shelter and I finished my reading book," Jack went on hurriedly.

"Oh, Jack, that's brilliant!" His mum shook her head. "Why didn't you say?"

"I've got another one." Jack sighed. "It's a non-fiction book about sharks. But it looks OK, I suppose."

He stuck the book in the pocket of his anorak when he set off with Mattie. He wanted to see if Daisy would listen to him reading again. If she came out from under the basket today, it would be like a scientific experiment, where you did the same thing again to make sure you got the same results twice.

He'd been a bit worried there would be lots of visitors looking at the dogs because it was a weekend – he didn't want a load of strangers hearing him reading. But when he asked, Mattie explained that they tried to encourage people to look at the dogs online first.

"It's upsetting for the dogs sometimes, having lots of people walking up and down and pointing at them," she told him as they hung up their coats in the little staffroom. "If they look at the dogs online, we can bring the ones they want to meet to the visitors' room, so they can get to know them."

Lucy and Adrian and Mattie were busy showing dogs and cats to people hoping to adopt, and whenever they had a spare minute they were working out a plan for a fundraising event at the shopping centre close to Jack's school. So no one noticed that when Jack had finished washing up the dogs' water bowls, he hurried round to Daisy's pen. Her tail was sticking out again, but he was sure the lump under the dog bed looked bigger. She was growing.

"I've got a new book," he explained, waving it at the wire front of the pen. "You probably don't know what sharks are, but they're interesting. They've been around for hundreds of millions of years – I never knew that till I got this book."

He settled down next to the pen and opened up the page about great whites. He started to read, glancing sideways hopefully every so often to see if Daisy was listening.

It took a little while, but by the time Jack was reading about shark attacks – there were only between five and ten attacks on humans every year, which he was surprised about – Daisy had poked her head out from under the bed to listen. When he had read the last of the photo captions on that page, Jack risked looking over at her.

"Hey…" he whispered. The puppy was peering at him, with her nose resting on her paws. When he spoke to her, he was sure he saw the dog bed bounce a little. Was she actually wagging her tail? He didn't want to put her off, so he quickly went back to reading out loud.

When Jack got to the end of the page, Daisy was sitting by the wire, watching him.

"Are you sure?" Amarah asked, looking up at Jack as he leaned over the fence between their gardens.

"Ummm. I think I'm sure. She didn't come out for Mattie or any of the staff at the shelter. I think she likes being read to. We're going over to the shelter in a minute, so you could come and see if she'll do it for you too? Mattie won't mind and Lucy will be OK if we take a note from your mum. We can help Mattie wash up bowls or do something else useful first."

Amarah nodded. "I'll go and see if it's OK." She raced off, but was back in a couple of minutes. "She said yes! Shall I climb over the fence?" Both gardens had benches in just the right place to make it easy to do. "Mum! I'm going now!" She hopped up on to the back of the bench and swung one leg over.

"I'll tell Mattie." Jack dashed into the house.

"Amarah wants to come too?" Mattie stared at him in surprise when he explained. "Why?"

"Because I told her all about Daisy and she wants to see her. We'll both help."

"Um, OK. But you have to be careful," Mattie said, smiling at Amarah as she came in through the back door. "Daisy's so shy, Amarah. We can't scare her. Though actually I noticed she was a bit braver yesterday when I took her dinner in. She looked at me! I know that doesn't sound like much, but it is."

Jack exchanged a hopeful glance with Amarah. It really sounded as if his reading was making Daisy feel better.

At the shelter, Lucy let them help groom two long-haired cats, and play with the black and white kittens that Jack had seen before. After that, though, they managed to hurry round to Daisy's pen before someone could give them another job to do.

The puppy was curled up on her side, but only half tucked under her bed this time – as though she wanted to be close enough to roll back underneath, just in case. She watched cautiously as Jack and Amarah approached her. Then instead of hiding away, she wriggled up on to her paws and came to stand by the wire.

"She never did that before!" Jack whispered.

"You'd better read to her," Amarah breathed. "She almost looks like she's waiting for you to start."

Jack sat on the floor and started to read the page in his book about sawfish. A couple of sentences in, Daisy sat down by the wire front of the pen and yawned.

"She definitely likes it," Amarah whispered and Jack nodded to her. It was almost relaxing, reading with Daisy listening. He'd been a bit worried that Amarah being there would make him feel awkward, but

Amarah was more interested in the dogs than she was in him. When he got to the end of the page, she waved a hand at him. "The others are listening too. Did you know?"

Jack glanced around at the rest of the pens. The dogs *were* all very quiet. Even Pug, who had the pen two down from Daisy, wasn't barking and whining the way he usually did. Jack held the book out to Amarah. "Here," he murmured. "You try. Read some of it to Pug – usually he's yapping all the time."

"OK…" Amarah took the book and sat down in front of Pug's pen. Jack could hear him panting as he came to the wire front to see what was going on. Then he started to bark. Amarah looked anxiously at Jack.

"Am I making him upset?"

"No, he barks a lot, honestly. Read to him. Let's see." Amarah started reading, gabbling nervously over Pug's barks at first, but then slowing down as she began to relax. Pug seemed to relax too. He stopped yapping and then he slumped down to the floor of the pen and started to chew on a rubber bone as he listened.

"It really does work," Jack said, looking around. Pug was chewing. Daisy had gone to lie down, but on top of her bed this time. Bertie, the big ginger Staffie mix, was slumped bonelessly on the floor of his pen, looking half asleep.

Amarah nodded. "They love it."

# Chapter Six

"She's got so much better."

Jack nodded, looking down proudly at Daisy. The little white puppy was standing on her hind legs, sniffing Lucy's fingers. It had been two weeks since Jack had first seen her, and Daisy hardly ever hid under her basket now – only when there was a lot of barking from the other dogs.

Lucy had let him go into the pen with Daisy a few times – after they'd checked with Mum – and it was a real treat, getting to stroke her and fuss over her. Her white fur looked as if it would be wiry, but she was incredibly soft, and her peachy ears were like warm velvet. Jack couldn't help imagining sitting on the sofa at home with her, stroking those ears while they watched TV.

"You wouldn't think she was the same dog," Mattie said, crouching down to let Daisy sniff her hands too, and Daisy wagged her tail wildly.

"She's still got a way to go, but she's getting really friendly." Lucy smiled at Jack. "Who knew reading to a dog could make such a difference!"

Jack beamed back at her. Since he'd discovered the secret – it still felt like a secret, an amazing discovery – he had been going back to the shelter with Mattie as often as he could. He could visit for a short while after school most weekdays and he got to be there for longer at the weekends. Since it was a Sunday, he'd been helping Lucy all afternoon, and she'd let him take some of the dogs into the little yard so he could throw toys for them to chase. It seemed like a lot of fun to Jack, but

Lucy promised it was really useful.

Jack did most of his reading with Daisy, but sometimes he read to the other dogs too. Pug was definitely less yappy after Jack had sat with him for a while – and it was helping Jack's reading too. Mr Gardner had told Mum that there had been *a definite improvement*.

Jack had even been doing extra reading online, trying to find out more ways to help Daisy. He and Amarah had found a shelter website that showed how to make a special treat mat, to keep bored dogs busy. Mattie had let him have the scruffy old fleece with holes in that she used to wear at the shelter. Mum had given her a new one for her birthday and Mattie had only been going to throw the old one away. He and Amarah had spent ages cutting up strips of fabric – Amarah's mum had given them one of Anika's polo shirts that was covered in whiteboard pen as well.

They'd tied the strips through the holes in the square of fleece, so it looked like a sort of fluffy doormat. Jack had finished it the night before and brought it with him to try out with Daisy when it was time for her dinner. If she liked it, he was thinking he could make some more, maybe one for every dog at the shelter.

"I'm going to help get your dinner ready now," he told Daisy after Lucy and Mattie had gone. He was kneeling on the floor outside her pen, so her nose was on a level with his if she stood on her back legs. He giggled as she swiped her tongue through the wire and licked him, and he had to wipe dog slobber off his cheek. "Uuurgh. I love you too. Back in a bit, OK?"

In the kitchen, Jack helped Mattie measure out the food, and then he took a handful of biscuits from Daisy's bowl and hid them one by one inside the fluffy mat. It was supposed to make eating more fun as the dogs snuffled out the food. It looked good, he thought, eyeing it proudly.

"You didn't say you'd finished it!" Mattie said, coming back in to grab more food bowls. "Are you going to try it out?"

"Yeah! Want to come and see?"

They headed back to Daisy's pen and Jack put her usual food bowl down first. He had a feeling that if she was really hungry, the treat mat might not be as much fun. If *he* was starving, having to search for his dinner would definitely make him grumpy. Then he left the mat in the corner of the pen and he and Mattie stood outside to watch.

Daisy wolfed down her food in about a minute, like she usually did, but she could clearly smell that there was more around somewhere. She sniffed her way over to the mat and started to root around in it eagerly, nosing out each biscuit and crunching it up. Jack could tell she really liked it – her tail was wagging excitedly and her ears were pricked right up.

"That's a hit," Mattie whispered.
"Wow, I thought it would take her
longer. She must have found nearly all
the food."

Daisy was slowing down now. She
nibbled one more treat out of the mat
and then slumped down next to it.
It looked as if she was trying to hold
the mat in her paws and cuddle it and
Mattie put her hand over her mouth to
stop herself laughing.

"She's going underneath it! Look!"
Jack nudged his sister and they

watched as Daisy snuffled her way under the treat mat, so that she was a little white dog with a fluffy blue head. "I think she's falling asleep. She still likes sleeping with something over her head, doesn't she?"

"Maybe she always will," Mattie said a little sadly. "I suppose dogs remember things they learn when they're little. It's a habit for her now." Then she put her arm round Jack and hugged him. "Sorry! I didn't mean to bring you down. She's always going to remember you reading to her as well, you know." Then she looked at her watch and made a face. "I'd better get on with feeding everyone now."

Jack crouched down, watching Daisy breathing gently as she slept. She was still so small, the mat could have covered her completely.

"Hey…" someone whispered next to him.

"Mum!" Jack jumped up. "I didn't even see you."

"I know! Sorry, I didn't mean to scare you. Time to head back home."

"Do we have to?" Jack sighed.

"Yes, it's nearly your dinner time as well!" Mum smiled at him. "I'm really impressed, you know. You've been spending so much time helping out here."

"I like it. I love dogs – I didn't know how much till I started coming here with Mattie."

Mum nodded. "I can see that." She took a deep breath. "Look, Jack, I've been thinking – would you like us to get a dog of our own?"

Jack stopped watching Daisy's soft, sleepy breathing and turned to stare at his mum. Did she mean it? They could have a dog? They could have Daisy?

He'd never even let himself hope that he could take her home. Earlier on, when Lucy had said how much better she was, he'd been so pleased. And then a little voice in his head had pointed out, *That means somebody could adopt her soon. Someone's going to take Daisy away. They might even change her name, and she wouldn't be your Daisy any more.* He'd squashed the voice down, and then Lucy had said she still had a way to go and the relief had just surged through him. *Not yet!*

"Yes!" he yelped and Daisy twitched under the treat mat. She wriggled and then her whiskery muzzle appeared and her dark eyes shone up at him from under the fluffy fabric. "I mean, yes, that would be amazing," he added in a quieter voice, grinning at Daisy. "She's—"

"I always thought it would be too difficult to cope with, but helping with the dogs here seems to have been so good for you. Of course, we'd have to make sure it was the right dog," Mum went on and Jack nodded. That made sense. Daisy was absolutely the right dog.

"Probably an older dog that's really calm? I expect Lucy could help us choose one."

Jack went on nodding for a second or two until he actually heard what Mum had said. *An older dog. Calm.*

"It wouldn't be good to have a puppy. We haven't got time to do a lot of training, when we're all so busy. But I could pop home from work at lunchtime to do a quick walk, and maybe Mattie could too sometimes."

Jack kept his eyes fixed on Daisy. He'd been so excited, so happy, for all of half a minute. How could only thirty seconds of hoping make everything seem so much worse now? It was as if he'd been given the most amazing present and then had it snatched away from him again. In fact, that was exactly what had happened.

From underneath the raggedy mat, Daisy watched Jack walk away, her ears drooping. He was going! He never went without saying goodbye to her. Even if he was on the other side of the wire, he always rubbed her ears and told her how beautiful she was.

She scrambled up, whining, but he didn't turn and run back. It was as if he couldn't even hear her. She whined louder, scrabbling her claws against the wire door, and then she gave a sharp little bark – but Jack disappeared round the corner of the passage without even looking back.

She stared out for a moment or two, her nose jammed in the gap between the wires. Then she turned away and picked up the treat mat in her teeth. It smelled of Jack – Jack and biscuits. Daisy took the mat with her as she crawled underneath her bed.

# Chapter Seven

"What's the matter with you?" Amarah hissed as Mr Gardner turned away.

Jack just shrugged.

"You knew how to do that sum, easy! Why didn't you do it?"

"Just leave me alone!" Jack stretched his legs out under the table and kicked Aaron's chair leg. And again. And then again.

"Oi! Stop it!" Aaron muttered. "I can tell it's you, Jack."

"Mr Gardner's watching you," Lily said in a sing-song voice. "You'll get into trouble!" She sounded quite excited about it.

Jack stopped kicking Aaron's chair and wrapped his feet round the legs of his own chair instead. He felt like he needed to glue himself down. It had been the same ever since yesterday. Mum and Mattie kept talking about dogs at the shelter, and which ones would make good pets. They both seemed really excited about it. Mum was even thinking about adopting Pug.

All he wanted to do was yell, *No! It has to be Daisy! I only want Daisy!* How could they even think he'd ever be happy with a different dog?

He made a strange noise, a sort of choking, gasping noise, and Amarah looked at him sharply. "Are you going to be sick?"

Jack shook his head, but he wasn't actually sure. He felt awful.

"Here." Amarah handed him her water bottle and he gulped from it gratefully. He wasn't going to be sick, it was just that he really, really wanted to cry, he realized. But he couldn't, not here, not in front of everybody.

"Is something wrong with Daisy?" Amarah whispered and Jack stared at her.

"How did you know?"

Amarah shrugged. "Hunch. You've been so much better at school since you started helping at the shelter and spending all that time with her. Now you've gone back to being weird and moody again."

"Who's Daisy?" Lily leaned over to ask. "Oooooh! Has Jack got a *girlfriend*?"

Amarah scowled at her. "Grow up," she snapped. "What are you, five?" and Lily went scarlet.

Jack put his hand over his mouth to stop himself laughing out loud. "Thanks," he muttered to Amarah. "My mum said we could adopt a dog."

Amarah shook her head. "I don't

get it! That's fantastic! Why are you upset?" Then she stared down at her maths like it was the most interesting thing she'd ever seen. "Mr Gardner's glaring at us," she said out the side of her mouth. "Tell me at break, OK?"

At break time, Amarah dragged Jack over to one of the benches and handed him half her banana. "I don't understand. I thought you really wanted a dog!"

Jack shook his head gloomily and squished the end of the banana between his fingers. He couldn't face eating it. "Nope. I want Daisy."

"So why can't you adopt her? Is she still too little? You could wait a bit, though, couldn't you?"

"It isn't that. Mum says we need to get an older dog that's calm. You know, well behaved. No puppies, because they're too hyper."

"What, so your mum doesn't want a dog version of you?" Amarah gave a snort.

Jack sighed. "Yeah."

"Sorry." Amarah's face fell. "That was meant to be a joke."

"It's true, though."

"But you've been loads better,"

Amarah pointed out. "Mr Gardner told your mum how good you've been. I heard him. That's all because of Daisy. Doesn't your mum understand that? Why didn't you tell her?"

"I don't know! I didn't think she'd listen. She said not a puppy." Jack handed the banana back to Amarah and wrapped his arms tightly round his middle, as if he was giving himself a hug.

"Yes, but Daisy's not just *any* puppy, is she?" Amarah shook her head. "You have to tell her. Didn't your sister say anything? Mattie knows how special Daisy is."

"Yeah..." Jack leaned back against the bench. "Maybe Mum would listen to Mattie," he admitted.

"Mattie, and me, and you," Amarah said firmly. "Your sister's taking you to the shelter again this afternoon, isn't she? So you have to explain everything to her. You can both tell your mum later, and I'll come round and tell her too."

Jack nodded slowly. Maybe Amarah was right – he *hadn't* told Mum how he felt about Daisy, he'd just expected her to know. He had to speak up.

Daisy's nose was just peeping out from under her bed, but she'd pulled the bed up close to the wire door so she could see what was happening. She was watching for Jack. Every time anyone had walked down the passage that day, she'd wriggled out a little more to see who it was. But it was never him. Daisy knew that usually Jack came later on, but still she couldn't help hoping. She was starting to feel hungry for dinner now, and he often arrived just before dinner time. Soon…

There was a scuffling, and footsteps, and Daisy scooted out from under the bed to look down the passage. There was a boy… Her ears pricked up hopefully.

No, not Jack yet. It was Lucy with a group of people Daisy didn't know.

"We do have one lovely young puppy actually, but she's a little nervous. I'm not sure she's ready for a busy family home just yet."

The group moved off towards the
main reception
area and Daisy
slumped down
on the floor
again. When
was he going
to come?
Then her tail
hunched between
her legs and a shudder ran over her.
What if he didn't come back? What
if he'd left her, like the people who'd
thrown her out of the car? Daisy was
almost sure that Jack was hers. But
they had been her people too.

She whimpered and scuffled the
blue treat mat under her paws to catch
the smell of food, and Jack, and home.

Jack ran down the passage to the corner where Daisy's pen was. He had a strange feeling in his stomach, as if she might have disappeared. All afternoon he'd been daydreaming – whenever Mr Gardner wasn't watching, anyway – thinking about what would happen after he'd explained to Mum. He *had* to make her understand. Amarah was right.

He'd imagined him and Daisy running round the park. Or Daisy asleep on his lap while he was doing his homework or watching TV. Maybe even asleep on the end of his bed. It all felt so real, it was too good to be true…

No, there she was, scrabbling wildly

at the side of her pen. She was so excited she was actually squeaking.

"Did you miss me?" Jack asked her, laughing. He caught her paws through the wire pen, hot little paws with hard black nails. "I missed you. Let me look at you…" It felt as if he was looking at her properly for the first time, now that there was a chance, just a chance, that she might be his dog.

She was so beautiful, even when she was jumping up and down and then darting off to whirl round her pen and flinging herself back to lick frantically at his fingers.

"Shhhh, shhh…" Jack said gently. "It's OK, Daisy. It's OK."

There were footsteps at the other end of the passage and he saw Lucy walking towards him with Mattie behind her. Lucy had a clipboard and a pen – she was tapping the pen against her teeth as if she was thinking.

"Hello! How's she doing, Jack?"

"Good. She was a bit excited, but she's calming down now." Jack looked back at Daisy, who was standing close to the wire, looking uncertain.

"I was just talking to a family who are looking for a puppy," Lucy explained. "Or a young dog anyway." She sighed. "I did try to suggest one of our lovely old-age pensioners, but they wanted a dog who'd be really active. Anyway –" she smiled at Jack – "I wondered about Daisy. What do you both think?" She looked round at Mattie. "You've done so much work socializing her, especially you, Jack. Do you think she'd cope with a family? It's actually only one boy and he's ten, so not too young."

Mattie nodded eagerly. "I think they'd have to take things slow, but yes. Daisy's such a gorgeous dog, she deserves a lovely home."

"No!" Jack yelped, and Daisy gave a worried whine and scraped one front paw against the concrete.

Mattie frowned at him. "Hey, gently."

"Sorry." Jack swallowed hard. He had to get this right. He had to make Lucy and Mattie understand – he'd meant to talk to Mum first, but he couldn't let Lucy give Daisy to somebody else. Not *his* dog. He crouched down and let Daisy snuffle at his fingers while he tried to think what to say.

"Did Mattie tell you that our mum said we could adopt a dog?" he asked Lucy.

She nodded, smiling. "Yes, it's brilliant news. I know Mattie's been desperate to have one for a while, and you're just such a dog person, Jack."

Jack tried to smile back, but his face felt stiff. "Maybe. I'm not sure if I'm really a dog person. It's … I mean … I only want Daisy!"

"Oh…" Mattie started to shake her head. "But Mum said…"

"I know," Jack broke in quickly. "We have to have a sensible dog. One of the old-age pensioners." He nodded at Lucy. "But Mum's saying that because I'm…" He faltered. "Um. Sometimes I'm not very sensible. Except I am. I could be. If it was Daisy. All that reading to her – I worked really hard – and she's so much better. We're *good* for each other."

Lucy beamed at him and reached down to pat his shoulder. "I know you are. You've been amazing with her and you can tell she's bonded with you." She glanced back at Mattie. "That was actually something I was a bit worried about – whether Daisy would ever build up such a good relationship with her new owner. But I couldn't stop Jack helping her, not when it was making such a difference."

Jack nodded eagerly. "Could you –
*please* could you tell my mum that?
That we don't need a sensible old dog?"
He looked hopefully at Mattie. "You
like her too, don't you?"

Mattie crouched down and looked
at the little white face peering back
at them anxiously through the wire.
"Silly question," she said lovingly, and
laughed as Daisy dabbed a cold black
nose against her hand. "OK. Now
we've just got to convince Mum."

# Chapter Eight

"I'm not at all sure about this." Jack's mum sighed. "A puppy! And a puppy who's had a hard time and isn't very reliable! That's exactly what I said I *didn't* want."

Mattie had called her mum and asked her to come by the shelter on her way home from work. Now Mum and Lucy and Mattie and Jack were all sitting in the visitors' room with Daisy. Jack had Daisy on his lap and she was half asleep, curled snugly against his school jumper. It was already covered in white hairs, but he didn't mind. He'd get them off with sticky tape if Mum was worried, but he loved it that Daisy had left a mark on him. It felt like he belonged to her.

Lucy nodded seriously. "I know exactly what you mean. But actually she's settling down amazingly well. She was very young when we got her, and yes she'd been abandoned and she was very withdrawn and nervous, but that's changed over the last few weeks. And I have to tell you, that's mostly down to Jack." She smiled at him and Jack grinned back at her shyly. He still wasn't used to people saying such nice things about him. "He's worked so hard. He's too young to be an official volunteer at the shelter like Mattie, but I'm really hoping he'll keep coming to help. Even when you have your own dog at home, Jack."

Jack nodded eagerly. "My friend Amarah wants to keep coming here as well," he told Lucy. "We wondered – do you think you could make it an official thing, us reading to the dogs? They all like it. And we thought maybe we could send a message to the schools around here, asking for more volunteers. So that there's someone reading to the dogs after school every day. Or some schools might walk children round to the shelter in their lunch break."

"Wow." Lucy blinked, looking surprised. "We could definitely think about it."

"It would mean more people coming to the shelter," Mattie pointed out. "We're always trying to think of ways to get more people in to see the dogs and cats."

Jack nodded. There were so many dogs who'd been at the shelter for a long time – they were desperate for proper homes. He ran one of Daisy's soft ears through his fingers and she snuffled sleepily.

"It would help with the children's reading as well," he added. "Schools would like that. I got loads better, just from reading out loud to Daisy and the others."

Lucy and Mum were nodding as if they agreed and Jack ducked his head to hide his proud grin. He was persuading them!

"That all sounds great," Jack's mum said slowly, "but I'm still worried about us adopting Daisy. How are we going to cope with a puppy?"

"It's tricky," Lucy admitted. "We usually say that someone needs to be home most of the time, to make sure young dogs aren't lonely."

"I can pop home from college if I have a free period," Mattie pointed out. "Most days I do. And you said you could come home at lunchtime, Mum. She'd get lots of little walks. Jack and I could take her out for a proper run before school."

"Amarah asked her mum this afternoon," Jack said eagerly. "She said she doesn't mind coming round to check on Daisy sometimes too. Daisy's so good, Mum, just look at her." He edged closer to his mum on the sofa and the puppy opened one eye lazily and yawned. "You could stroke her?" he suggested.

Mum reached out one hand and ran it gently down Daisy's back. "She's very soft," she told Jack, smiling. "Hello, sweetheart…" she added as Daisy wriggled round and licked the back of her hand. "You are very cute, aren't you? And I can see how much she loves you both. Maybe it would be all right." Then she gave a surprised laugh as Daisy wobbled upright and

stomped over on
to her lap instead.
The little white
dog slumped
down again with
a massive yawn
and seemed to go
back to sleep. "Oh …
I wasn't expecting that."
Mum rubbed Daisy's ears, and
looked up at Jack and Mattie. "I think
she might have decided for us…"

Daisy wriggled a little in Jack's arms,
turning so she could gaze up at him.
He looked afraid and she could smell
the worry rising off him. She pressed

her nose gently into the gap under his chin and felt him catch his breath in a half laugh. "Thanks," he whispered, rubbing his cheek against the top of her head. "This is really scary."

Daisy felt him step forward and then Amarah held up a piece of paper in front of her nose. Daisy leaned out of Jack's arms to sniff it and then she nibbled the bottom corner. The crowd of people in front of them laughed and Daisy beat her tail against Jack's arm. She didn't know what was happening, but she liked the noise. Jack started to read out loud.

"Thank you for coming to the fundraiser for Tall Pines Animal Shelter. Today we are launching a new scheme to help animals, and children…"

Daisy sighed happily, resting her nose on his shoulder.

"I started to read to my dog Daisy when she was still at Tall Pines, after being abandoned. I didn't know the amazing effect reading to dogs could have. Please help us…"

"You did so well!" Mattie hugged Jack, trying not to squash Daisy, and Daisy squirmed delightedly. "I could hear people in the crowd saying how gorgeous Daisy is."

"I can't believe I read in front of all those people," Jack murmured. He was still feeling a bit shaky.

"I can't believe you did either. You were brilliant." Mattie stroked Daisy's nose. "And so were you, little one."

"Lucy says lots of people are asking about making appointments to visit," Amarah told them excitedly, pointing at the board behind Jack, which was plastered with big photos of the dogs at the shelter. "Someone wants to come and see Pug! She said she's always had pugs and he's really beautiful!"

"I'd better go and help write down some details," Mattie said, darting away, and Jack sat down on the edge of the little platform. Daisy wriggled out of his arms and started to sniff around their feet. The shopping centre was full of intriguing smells.

"How are you doing?" Amarah asked, sitting next to him. "I was a bit worried you might run away just before it was your speech."

"Me too." Jack shivered. "But it was OK. It sounded like I was talking to the crowd, but actually I just read it to Daisy."

Daisy heard her name and looked round. Then she jumped up next to him again, squishing in between Jack and Amarah and nosing lovingly at both of them. She sank down with her muzzle on Jack's knee and gazed up at him with huge dark eyes.

"Do you want to go home?" Jack whispered to her. "Me too. It's OK, Daisy, we'll be home soon, I promise."

Daisy thumped her tail lazily against Amarah's legs and then wriggled further up so she was slumped half on to Jack's lap. She didn't mind where they went, as long as Jack came with her.

# Out Now

From MULTI-MILLION best-selling author
*Holly Webb*

# The Smallest Kitten

*Illustrated by Sophy Williams*

# Out Now

From MULTI-MILLION best-selling author

*Holly Webb*

# The Borrowed Puppy

Illustrated by Sophy Williams

# HOLLY WEBB

Holly Webb started out as a children's
book editor and wrote her first series for
the publisher she worked for. She has been
writing ever since, with over one hundred
books to her name. Holly lives in Berkshire,
with her husband and three children.
Holly's pet cats are always nosying around
when she is trying to type on her laptop.

For more information
about Holly Webb visit:

## www.holly-webb.com